*Good*

*Some Little Danger*

*basicly boy meets girl*

# Get Your
# Coventry Romances
# Home Subscription NOW

## And Get These
## 4 Best-Selling Novels
## *FREE:*

### *LACEY*
by Claudette Williams

### *THE ROMANTIC WIDOW*
by Mollie Chappell

### *HELENE*
by Leonora Blythe

### *THE HEARTBREAK TRIANGLE*
by Nora Hampton

# THE
# RANDOM
# GENTLEMAN

*a novel by*

# Elizabeth Chater

FAWCETT COVENTRY • NEW YORK

THE RANDOM GENTLEMAN

Published by Fawcett Coventry Books, a unit of CBS Pub-
lications, the Consumer Publishing Division of CBS Inc.

ISBN: 0-449-50210-4

Printed in the United States of America

First Fawcett Coventry printing: September 1981

10  9  8  7  6  5  4  3  2  1

*To Eve Lynn*
*wise and wonderful*

# Chapter 1

The Honorable Belinda Sayre tapped gently on the door of the library and was bidden to enter by a bellow from the voice which had made subalterns tremble when General the Right Honorable the Earl of Sayre had commanded his troops in the field. Not the least daunted, Belinda pushed open the door and stood upon the threshold, looking, as she was well aware, an enchanting picture of feminine loveliness. The rich golden hair which her admiring swains had likened to sunlight, guinea gold, and once, lamentably (but he was after all a younger son), to butter, was shining smooth and charmingly arranged by her devoted dresser. Her costume was perfect for a quiet morning in an elegant London town house, and her manner, at once merry and modest, was exactly calculated to win over the crustiest elderly martinet who ever huffed and puffed at a beloved granddaughter.

"You sent for me, Grandpapa?"

As expected, the parade-ground roar moderated to an indulgent purr as My Lord Sayre's aging eyes took in the delectable vision in the doorway. "Come in, come in, Puss! Close the door behind you! I've a private and important matter to discuss with you, and don't wish to be interrupted."

Big pansy-brown eyes regarded him with a naughty twinkle. "What is this so-important matter, Grandpapa? Has some great nobleman asked you for my hand? Or has that horrid Lady Wegg come tattling to you about my behavior at the ball last evening?"

The craggy eyebrows came down over the sharp old eyes. "Now what have you been up to, naughty Puss? Agatha Wegg has said nothing. Sent her away with a bee in her bonnet last time she came here talebearing! Woman's a scandalmonger, and so I told her."

"I knew I could count upon you, Grandpapa! Sound as a nut!" said Belinda, making eloquent play with her big brown eyes.

Her grandfather was not beguiled. "Asked what you'd been up to, Miss," he repeated, sternly. "No mealymouthed maunderings, if

8

you please! The plain truth with no bark on it."

Belinda sighed dramatically. "Well, it seems I had inadvertently promised the same dance to three gentlemen—and they got rather angry at one another." She peeped at the old man from under her long, silky lashes. "They went outside and—ah—engaged in fisticuffs." Observing the mounting displeasure in the fierce old face, she said quickly, "I do not think many people knew of it. Major Cholmondeley went out after them and—ah—broke it up. Sent them all home. They were all of them officers under his command."

"Chum ought to keep his young fire-eaters on a tighter rein," snapped the Earl. "In *my* day, an officer would never have so far forgotten himself as to start a mill at a private ball." He snorted. *"Three* of them? It was a three-way mill?"

"I don't know," confessed Belinda. "I was dancing with Lord Everleigh, and didn't hear of it until later."

"Everleigh? Don't wish you to be seen showing complaisance to that ne'er-do-well! Next thing to a gazetted fortune hunter!"

"Is he?" asked Belinda with interest. "He is very entertaining."

"Bound to be," grunted her grandfather. "His stock in trade—cozening tricks and wheedles! Depend on it, Puss, he's after your fortune."

A small frown marred the delicate smoothness of Belinda's forehead. At eighteen years of age, and thoroughly enjoying the delights of a most successful First Season, it is not flattering to suspect that some part of one's success may be attributable to the enormous fortune left by one's father, killed at Waterloo. Her only memory of the gallant Major the Right Honorable Henry Sayre, Viscount Melville, was of a tall man in an elaborate uniform, who swung his small daughter up into his arms, kissed her, and then gave her to her grandfather with the husky injunction to "Look after the child, sir!"

After the death of first, her mother, and later, her father, the Earl had indeed done his best to look after her, and Belinda, though she often teased him, knew and reciprocated the deep love he felt for her.

"Are they all, Grandpapa? After my fortune, I mean?"

"Of course not, Puss. Think I'd let you mingle with that sort of scaff and raff? Thing is, some such fellows bound to work their way into even the best houses. But none of that matters."

Belinda looked her bewilderment.

Her grandfather seemed to be encountering some difficulty in explaining his odd statement.

"Cut line, Grandpapa," Belinda advised with a smile.

"How many times must I tell you, Miss, that such cant is odious upon the lips of a well-brought-up young lady?" he shouted. Then, catching her slanted smile, he grinned reluctantly. "I know! You will say you heard me say it, so of course it must be quite acceptable! Minx! Well, suppose I must tell you. Reason I sent for you. Your—your fiancé is returning to London today. You are to meet him at his sister's Grand Ball this evening, and your engagement is to be announced at a dinner party here the day after tomorrow."

He stared at her with would-be fierceness under his shaggy white eyebrows. His granddaughter was looking dazed—as well she might, and her expression gradually became anxious. She moved closer and placed one small hand upon his arm.

"Dearest Grandy," (a term sne nad not used since early childhood) "are you sure you are feeling quite the thing? Do let me call your batman! Sit down, dearest, do!"

The old man patted her arm tenderly, his face turning a dull red. "No, no, child, I'm quite fit! Perhaps we should both sit down, and I'll explain."

As she seated herself near him, the girl's anxious look was gradually being replaced by something her grandfather liked even less.

"Now what is this about, sir? Engagement announced? Fiancé? I think you had better open the budget!"

The Earl, feeling more nervous than ever he had upon the eve of battle, touched his forehead lightly with his immaculate handkerchief, cleared his throat, wished for a strong whiskey, and then, aware of the minatory glance being leveled at him by his granddaughter, squared his shoulders and began to speak.

"Y'r father's best friend, as you may often have heard me say, was the young Duke of Romsdale. Thor Dane and Henry formed a lasting friendship in childhood and, after attending the same schools, joined the army in the same regiment. They married in the same year, and when Thor's son was born, they decided that, if Henry should have a daughter, she must marry young Osric." He coughed, and became even redder under the girl's shocked look. "Had to wait ten years for you to be born, Miss, and many's the time they almost gave up in despair. Then your dear Mother bore you—and all was well at last!"

He paused and mopped his forehead again.

Belinda was glaring at him. "Gothic! Perfectly gothic! I cannot believe...but of course it is just such an addlebrained scheme as two young men, comrades-at-arms, might concoct in the night watches before a battle. But that *you*, Grandpapa, and the Duke's father, should have permitted such a mawkish ploy—!"

"Permitted? Thor's father and I agreed

wholeheartedly! Excellent stock on both sides, a balance of property—"

"It seems both the families were fortune-hunting," said Belinda sharply. "There is little to choose between such mercenary matchmaking and the maneuverings of poor Lord Everleigh!" Another unwelcome thought struck her. "Are you telling me that this Osbert—"

"Osric! Osric!" interjected her harassed grandfather.

*"Osric!"* the girl pronounced the name with awful scorn. "And where, pray, has this weak-kneed paragon been hiding himself? Couldn't you bring him up to scratch? I have heard of no Osric Dane in London! Does he bury himself in the country?"

Her grandfather's bellow of rage cut across her sarcasm. "Enough, Miss! Young Dane has had a distinguished career both in the army and in government, but it has not been in England! He was in Henry's regiment at Waterloo. It was he who brought back your dear father's effects to us. His own father having been killed at Salamanca, he had already, at eighteen, assumed his position as Duke of Romsdale. He was seconded to Castlereagh at the Congress of Vienna, and thus began a remarkable career in diplomacy. He's represented England abroad in a most distinguished way these ten years! And you, Miss, have not heard of him because the set of silly

13

fribbles you go about with during the Season are such lightweights that they take no thought for politics, diplomacy, or our country's destiny!"

This last insult was more than a spirited female could endure. "'Silly fribbles'? When you've practically *forced* me into the *ton,* placed me under the chaperonage of Lady Tulliver, induced Lady Freya Goncourt to sponsor me, *and* insisted upon my accepting every invitation which was delivered to this house—!"

This attack was too formidable and too accurate for the aging nobleman to counter with logic. He resorted to his parade-ground voice. "Silence, Miss! Done my best for the orphaned grandchild left in my care! If I have made mistakes—" he paused, peering under his heavy brows and assuming an expression of sorrowful remorse. His voice softened. "If I have failed—" he sighed with histrionic grief.

"Gammon!" snapped his too-perceptive grandchild. "You'll catch cold trying that tune with me! You are the most *managing,* overbearing tyrant it has ever been my misfortune to encounter! Now tell me exactly what is planned for me with this paragon, this young plenipotentiary—probably a pompous, arrogant, stiff-rumped—"

"Belinda!" shouted the Earl, affronted beyond bearing by her use of words he himself

14

had taught her. "You had better mind your tongue, or no man, not even Lord Everleigh, will offer for you!" Then, observing the sudden light of interest on the lovely, expressive little countenance, he added harshly, "Would have hoped that a granddaughter of mine would honor her father's sacred oath—!"

Belinda, who thought this was hitting below the belt—her grandfather was an addict of fisticuffs, and had described to her many a fine mill he had witnessed—was nevertheless constrained to agree that she could not totally disregard her dead father's carefully arranged plan for her. She was understood to say that she supposed she would have to meet the creature, at least. "But sir," she continued, "have we not already accepted the invitation of Lady Freya Goncourt for a ball this evening?"

"Gal's Osric's sister," her grandfather informed her. "Married that French émigré fellow. Widowed."

"But I *like* her!" began the girl, annoyed to find herself feeling kindly toward anyone in the haughty Osric's family.

"Might like him, too, once you meet him," suggested the Earl. "They tell me he's a deuced good-looking man. Got the females after him in swarms," he offered hopefully.

"Indeed?" retorted Belinda icily. "What a charming prospect for the lady unfortunate enough to be his wife! The thought of sharing even such an abundance of male beauty and charm is repugnant to me! Every feeling must be lacerated!" Then, leaving her high flight and descending to her normal style, "I'm damned if I'll meet him!"

"Belinda!" groaned the Earl, reduced to despair.

After a severe glance, the girl relented a little. "I'll agree to meet this Nonpareil tonight, but only because I like his sister very much, and because you and my father committed me at least to considering him. But I warn you, he will have to be something quite out of the ordinary before I will accept this gothic arrangement of yours."

"You are a disrespectful baggage," snapped her grandfather, then added with a groan, "and I only hope the fellow will make you happy!"

Mollified by his evident concern, Belinda kissed his cheek, and told him he was a wicked schemer, but she forgave him.

# Chapter 2

Looking dazzlingly fair in white satin embroidered with tiny golden rosebuds, a wide golden sash clasping her small waist, and a soft frill of lace framing her golden head, Belinda mounted the wide stairway that evening on her grandfather's arm. At the top, Lady Freya Goncourt greeted her guests with the charm which had made her one of the Season's first hostesses. She held out both hands to Belinda when it was their turn to be received.

"My dear Belinda, how enchantingly pretty you are looking this evening! And Lord Sayre! How good of you to come! A dreadful squeeze, I am afraid, but then we shall have other times to enjoy a comfortable coze!" and her smiling eyes invited them to share her pleasure at the projected union of the two families.

"Did everyone know of it but me?" muttered Belinda to her grandfather. She was about to move on into the reception rooms when Lady Freya bent toward her.

"I am charged to make Osric's apologies," she whispered. "His Majesty sent for him an hour ago to discuss some point of Foreign Office policy. He should be back any moment. It is vexatious," she added, "but one cannot refuse when royalty requests."

"I quite undersatand," soothed Belinda, but a little frown set itself between her brows. Surely, if this Osric was as deft at diplomacy as Grandpa implied, he could manage one fat, selfish old man, even if he was the King!

She set herself to enjoy the ball, and within five minutes had every dance promised, to her grandfather's chagrin. However, he said nothing, trusting that His Grace of Romsdale would be clever enough to remedy the situation when he appeared. Belinda seemed to be enjoying herself very much—at least her cheeks were charmingly flushed and her eyes very bright. The Earl wondered wistfully if he might take himself off to the card room for a few relaxing hands of whist, but decided to wait in the ballroom until His Grace had made his entrance.

By the time supper was announced, without the arrival of the guest of honor, whispered comments were being exchanged in corners and on the dance floor. The Earl sought out his granddaughter among the dancers, and then wished he had not. For upon her beautiful little face was an expression he had learned to dread during her childhood—her mulish look, he characterized it with less grace than truth.

Belinda was in fact very angry. She had thought well of herself for coming to meet this Osric halfway. Perhaps he might share her annoyance at the foolish pact their fathers had made; they could laugh a little and set all to rights. Perhaps he might prove to be an interesting man, older and more knowledgeable than the love-smitten youths who formed her court, and they might decide to explore the possibilities offered by the engagement. Certainly he would count himself fortunate to be affianced to the acknowledged Belle of the Season! But none of these resolutions to the problem could be explored until the wretched man presented himself—and he had not done so! As the evening proceeded, Belinda began to catch the faintly malicious murmurings which linked her name with that of the absent guest of honor. The final straw was put in place by Belinda's archrival, Miss Dulcinia Wegg, whose mamma was the intelligencer whose tongue wagged so frequently at Belinda's expense. The odious Dulcinia—a black-haired beauty, divinely tall—accosted her rival in front of two of the Season's prime catches, Milords Lacey and Daughton.

"What is this I hear about an engagement between yourself and dear Freya's brother?" asked the brunette beauty.

"I am sure I don't know," smiled Belinda. "What *do* you hear? Perhaps you should ask your mamma? She is never at a loss for the latest *on-dit*."

This shrewd thrust was received with bright-eyed amusement by the two young men, and a tight-lipped smile from Dulcinia.

"I was sure the gossip must be mistaken," she came back smoothly, "for it seems to me the gentleman is most anxious not to show his face, and since he is the guest of honor, one would say he must have a powerful reason to serve his sister so!"

"Perhaps the poor old fellow was exhausted, and had to take to his bed," was the best Belinda could come up with. "Older men tire easily, you know. My grandfather dozes off every night after dinner."

Most fortunately the music struck up at this moment, and Belinda was carried off by Lord Daughton to waltz in the ballroom. The young nobleman, proud of his partner, thought he had never seen the exquisite little creature in better looks. He told her so, and his warm admiration did much to restore her damaged spirits. So much, in fact, that she went to find her grandfather immediately after the dance was ended and informed him that she was suffering from a migraine and wished to return home at once.

The Earl opened his mouth to protest, caught the look on his beloved grandchild's face, and capitulated at once. Offering her his arm, he led her quietly to the cloakroom, made their excuses to Lady Freya, accepted her anguished apologies courteously, and sent a footman after their carriage. By the time Belinda appeared at the front door in her modish velvet cloak, her grandfather was able to lead her down to their carriage and help her into it.

Their journey home was silent.

# Chapter 3

The following morning, after a very restless night, Belinda was unlucky enough to come down to the breakfast parlor just as two callers were arriving at the front door. The butler followed her into the parlor with their names, and Belinda heard with a sinking heart that Miss Dulcinia Wegg and Miss Sylphe Courtney wished to be received by his mistress.

In very pride, Belinda was compelled to receive them. She offered them a cup of coffee with as good a grace as she could muster. Dulcinia's sharp eyes had already assessed the dark shadows under her rival's eyes; she was all pretty concern for dear Belinda's health. That young lady fended off their condolences with poise and was holding her own very nicely until Dulcinia dropped her bombshell.

"Oh, by the way, Belinda, you and your grandfather left too early last night. The dear Duke arrived and put new life into the party! Such a divinely handsome man! So youthful when one considers the honors that have been heaped upon him! The word is that His Majesty is to bestow an additional peerage upon Osric, as I am sure you must have known! But of course we must not speak of it until it is official!"

Oh, must we not? thought Belinda. How did *you* get into this? But she said nothing, merely smiled as though she had known it all the time.

This deception was not permitted by her determined adversary. The next attack was an oblique one. "Osric has such a droll wit!" she began, laughing lightly. "He had us in stitches! When I told him what you had said about him being exhausted and needing to rest in bed like your grandfather, he was most amused! He said—so wittily!—that to a schoolroom chit, twenty-eight years must seem quite aged; and then he went on to inform us that in Italy, where he has just been stationed to negotiate a most important treaty, the name Belinda means a snake! We all were quite carried away with his droll comments!"

"What were they?" inquired Belinda, as

though eager to hear and be amused. "Can you remember any of them?"

"But I just *told* you—" began Dulcinia, and then stopped speaking to glare at Belinda.

"You thought it was witty to say my name meant a snake? Well, perhaps it was the *way* he said it," excused Belinda, neatly taking the wind out of the other girl's sails.

Very soon after this unsatisfactory encounter, the two visitors left, and Belinda lost no time in going to her grandfather's bookroom. With red flags of outrage flying in her white face, and great brown eyes hard with humiliation, the girl informed her grandparent what Dulcinia had told her. "And if you think I am going to be seated at our dinner table beside a man who called me a snake in public, you are much mistaken!"

"But the dinner is to announce your engagement!" protested the bewildered Earl. "Everyone's been asked, and accepted! Even His Majesty was pleased to consent—!"

"You will of course do as you wish," said this new, cold-eyed young woman. "I would not attend if my life depended on it!"

"Belinda—the girl got it wrong. Perhaps she made it all up. You know what the mother is like! But you are the hostess tomorrow night. It would offer a great insult to His Majesty—to all our guests—if you failed to appear. You can carry it off, child! You must do so—for your own sake! When I announce your engagement, it will give the lie to that little vixen's spiteful gossip!"

"No," said Belinda. "This is intolerable! Not even you, Grandpapa, could expect me to endure such an odious situation. To be paraded before this arrogant, complacent, finicking—*backbiting* lordling as though I were a blood mare he might consider adding to his stable—!"

"Belinda! You go too far with your plain-speaking!" The Earl bristled at her, his brown eyes glaring from under bushy white eyebrows. "All the man said was that your name means a snake in Italian—"

"*All!* And he said it with a laugh, in front of Dulcinia Wegg and Sylphe Courtney and who knows how many more—and they all laughed! Does it please you to know that your precious Osric made me a joke in public?" The girl glared back at her grandfather with eyes so dark with anger and chagrin that they seemed almost black. "You know the Weggs! The mother will have it all over Town that he called me a snake! I shall be a laughing-stock!"

The Earl frowned. "Osric Dane is a diplomat and a friend of our family. It is surely unlike him to speak so. I cannot think what would have caused him to be so indiscreet—if in fact he was."

Belinda had neglected to mention her own sneer at the Duke's old age and exhaustion,

26

and she did not repair the omission now. Instead she offered, "He is likely as reluctant for this match as I am. I wager he thinks that if he insults me publicly enough, even you will be willing to cry off!"

The Earl slammed his fist down on the desk, making the papers on it flutter. "That is the second time you have said 'even you' in that tone of voice, Miss! It could be that the Duke has heard of your outspokenness, your defiance of restraint! Your success during the Season has spoiled you, child, given you an inflated idea of your consequence. You are my ward, and you will do whatever I decide. Let us hope Dane has not taken a disgust of you from your unmaidenly behavior! However, I expect he will honor his obligation. And I will not allow a hoydenish miss to overset a plan which Dane's father and yours agreed upon when you were both in your cradles—"

This harsh speech from her normally doting grandparent threw Belinda into a fine temper. The thought that the rude, arrogant Osric would condescend to "honor his obligation" to a hoyden put her into a passion.

"Cradles!" she snapped rudely. "You must be all about in your head, sir! The creature is at least ten years older than I am, and if he was still in his cradle when I was, I wonder at your desiring the connection with such a looby!" Entertained by the picture of the high-in-the-instep nobleman as a ten-year-old in a crib, the girl broke into harsh laughter.

Her grandfather thrust himself out of his chair in a towering rage. "You know he was in school then! By God, Belinda, if you were a boy I'd have you whipped! Is this the way you have been talking in society? If so, it is no wonder he called you a schoolroom chit! He's a man of proven worth. He was successful at Oxford, a fine and gallant soldier, and one of England's biggest assets abroad—!"

Another peal of ironic laughter from his recalcitrant grandchild at this rather infelicitous phrase gave him pause. His fierce old eyes took in the ravaged pride in the girl's countenance, the hurt in the big pansy-brown eyes. Changing his tactics, the Earl said more gently, "It's not like you, Bel, to prejudge a man. You've never met Dane, never spoken to him. How can you rate him so harshly?"

"Don't try to turn me up soft, Grandpapa! You raised me, and I know your tricks. But you know me, too, and you cannot wish me to sit at table with the man who has made a public mock of me, while all London laughs and whispers that the Duke of Romsdale finds himself compelled to offer for—a snake!"

There was so much real distress in the girl's lovely face that the Earl's domineering old heart nearly misgave him. He adored his orphaned granddaughter, knew himself to be quite besotted over the child, but—damn it

28

all!—the girl's father had designed the match, and it was a splendid one in every way. No ignorant slip of a girl could be permitted to cast aside a secure, honored future on the excuse of a malicious scrap of gossip! Finding himself thus reassured by his own evaluation of the situation, the Earl said in a loud, blustering tone, "Let me hear no more of these missish vaporings, Belinda! You are a female, and too young to know what's best for you. You will be guided by me, child. You will attend our dinner party tomorrow night, wearing your prettiest dress, and you will conduct yourself in a modest, well-bred manner which will silence the malicious tittle-tattle your behavior of last night has caused. Do you understand me?" and the old martinet glared at her from under his shaggy eyebrows.

*"Grandy!"* cried the girl with inarticulate appeal.

Softened a little by her obvious distress, the old man went on in a gentler voice, "Depend on it, having missed you last night at his sister's ball, Dane will wait upon you today. Sure to! With flowers, and some little frippery to win a smile from you—possibly with an explanation, an apology—" His invention failed, but he finished with a firmness Belinda had come to recognize over the years. "Now, child, you will allow yourself to be guided by those who know a good deal more of the world than you can yet do! Choose your loveliest dress for tomorrow night, and prepare yourself to entertain the King, our friends, and your fiancé with your most charming behavior!"

He waved his hand in dismissal, satisfied that he'd set the child straight, and calmed the little tempest in a teapot. As Belinda went quietly from the library, he congratulated himself on his firm control of what might have worked into a most distasteful situation. He would have been considerably less smug had he been able to read the hurt and anger in Belinda's rebellious heart. Perhaps she had been spoiled by the remarkable success of her first season in the Beau Monde, and the enthusiastic court paid her by a number of dashing young peers, but she was very young and very vulnerable to the kind of sophisticated, sneering irony which had been reported to her this morning. She had made up her mind that the arrogant Duke of Romsdale could entertain himself when he came to dinner at Sayre House tomorrow night.

# Chapter 4

Somewhat to the Earl's chagrin, no flowers arrived for Belinda from the Duke, either that day or the following morning. Even more disturbing, there was neither visit nor message from His Grace. At luncheon the day of the dinner party to announce the engagement, Lady Tulliver was the only one at the table to be in high spirits, chatting on endlessly about the arrangements she had made. Belinda presented herself for the meal looking pale and subdued. To her grandfather's efforts at conversation she replied with quiet courtesy and none of her usual sparkle. The Duke's name was not mentioned. Belinda herself said nothing about that evening's party.

After lunch, trying in vain to get a few minutes' nap in his bookroom, the Earl wondered if perhaps he should have sent some sort of message to his guest of honor, but consoled himself with the fact that Lady Freya had been all too conscious of the effect upon Belinda of the Duke's unintended slight, and would bring her brother up to the mark tonight. Anything else was unthinkable—an insult he could not accept, however strong his desire to carry out the expressed wish of his dead son.

That evening, about one hour before the guests were expected to arrive, General the Right Honorable James Henry Darell ffoulkes Sayre, seventh Earl of Sayre and Wendover, marched down the broad central stairway of Sayre House looking every inch the gallant old soldier, shoulders squared, back erect, orders and decorations shining. The first person he saw in the splendid reception area was his butler, Farwell, who made it obvious that he wished to address his master.

"Well, Farwell, what is it?"

"It's Miss Belinda, My Lord," uttered Farwell in accents of doom. "Lady Tulliver is quite beside heself—it seems Miss Belinda is not in the house—"

*"Not?* Then where the devil is the girl?" roared the old martinet.

"I could not say, My Lord." The old

butler knew the signs and offered no provocation.

"Where is Lady Tulliver?"

"In the Gold Salon, My Lord."

The Earl stormed into the elegant room. Lady Tulliver was indeed there, draped out on a satin sofa, attended by at least three female servants, one of whom was revealed to be Mrs. Munn, the housekeeper. The odor of burnt feathers tainted the air. The Earl's bellow of rage shocked the two weeping maids into little shrieks of alarm, but Mrs. Munn, long in the Earl's service, was made of sterner stuff.

"Miss Belinda has left the house, My Lord," she said crisply, "and Lady Tulliver has swooned."

The Earl gathered his forces. "How do you know the girl's gone?" he snapped.

"There was a letter," the housekeeper informed him.

"By God, there would be!" shouted the Earl. "Where is this—this missive?"

Lady Tulliver, opening one eye, fumbled in her corsage and extended a shaking hand in which she clutched a crumpled sheet of notepaper. The Earl took it and and stalked over the the mantelpiece to read it in the light of the numerous candles burning there.

Dear Lady Tulliver (the message read, in Belinda's unmistakable hand): I am

33

compelled to leave Sayre House before the Dinner Party. My Grandfather knows my reasons. Give him my dearest love. I shall let him know where I am as soon as I can. My apologies for making your numbers uneven at the table tonight.

Belinda

When the Earl raised his head, Mrs. Munn, who knew, after the manner of all good servants everywhere, every detail of the imbroglio, was seized with a sense of pity. The face was ravaged, and the look in the fierce old eyes caused her to avert her own gaze from such naked suffering.

A moan from the supine lady upon the sofa drew everyone's attention. "Where can she be?" Lady Tulliver cried, weak-voiced. "The *King—!*"

"Someone must—that is, I must inform His Majesty, of course—but are you sure the child isn't hiding somewhere, just to—to teach us a lesson?"

Mrs. Munn was embarrassed. She had never seen the Earl in such straits in all the forty years she had served his house. She waited a moment for Lady Tulliver to speak, but when the only sounds from that woman were renewed sobs, Mrs. Munn said calmly, "No, My Lord, she is not hiding anywhere in this house. I sent maids to search as soon as

Her Ladyship informed me of the—the problem." When the Earl was about to speak, she held up one hand, and continued, "I then inquired of the footmen, and learned that Miss Belinda had summoned a hackney coach about three o'clock this afternoon, which took her to the Saracen's Head Inn, where there is a stagecoach office. Farwell informs me that the second footman, James, who handed Miss Belinda into the coach, overheard her giving the driver her direction. James went immediately to Aldgate High Street to the inn to make inquiries."

"Damme, that's good staff-work!" congratulated the Earl, for the first time feeling that all might not be lost. "What was her destination, Mrs. Munn?"

"That, James did not discover, My Lord," admitted the housekeeper, "since he ran to the inn rather than securing a hackney, and so missed your granddaughter at the posting station. He was subsequently unable to ascertain which stagecoach she had taken."

At that disappointing moment, Farwell entered the Gold Salon, flinging back the doors with a flourish. "His Grace the Duke of Romsdale; the Lady Freya Goncourt!" Then, catching sight of the still-recumbent Lady Tulliver, the old fellow gulped audibly, and said "My Lord!" in a strangled voice.

* * *

His Grace had been feeling unaccountably ill at ease as he accompanied his sister into the somber elegance of Sayre House. The evening to come presented itself to his mind as one fraught with as many challenges and hidden traps as the most ticklish of diplomatic crises. He was buoyed up by the consciousness that his own behavior in this vexatious business—pitchforked as he had been into a connection with a gauche schoolroom miss!—had been, in fact, exemplary. The truth of the matter was that His Grace had been even more courted and spoiled by adulation than had Belinda Sayre. A gallant, dashing, and courageous officer at eighteen; the youngest and most brilliant of Castlereagh's negotiators at the Congress of Vienna and after, he had gone on to win a firm place in the diplomatic corps of his country. Since he was over six feet tall, golden-haired, and extraordinarily handsome, his diplomatic success was more than matched by his social triumphs in the sophisticated, glittering capitals of Europe. Possessed of a fine old name, an enormous fortune, and natural ability which gave him preeminence in sports, he was widely regarded as a Nonpareil, and had come to have a very high opinion of his own worth.

And now to discover himself pledged to marry a green girl with a pert tongue and no sense of dignity—! It did not bear thinking of! He had refused to consider his sister's gentle suggestions that a gift of flowers would remove Belinda's pique at his nonappearance at the ball, and that a visit of courtesy to the girl would change his own opinion. In fact, he had informed Freya arrogantly, if that wily old campaigner hadn't already wheedled royalty into attending his wretched dinner party, Dane might have managed to get himself out of the whole disastrous business with the exertion of just a little diplomacy.

The King, of course, like all notorious philanderers, was sickeningly sentimental about everyone else's matrimonial prospects, and had spent quite a third of the time at the ill-timed conference on the night of Freya's ball in congratulating the Duke on his approaching marriage to a demmed handsome little filly.

"Got all the young bucks panting after her, my boy! She may be a bit hot-at-hand, Osric, and she will need a firm hand on the reins," with a leer, "which you, from all I can hear, will surely be able to provide!"

Now, entering the impressive portals of Sayre House with Freya, the Duke was in such a recalcitrant mood that he said, quite loudly, as he allowed the butler to take his evening cape and gloves, *"Abandon Hope, all ye who enter here!"*

Lady Freya, who had been unusually quiet during the drive, did not respond with the laugh he had come to expect when he was pleased to utter a witticism. Instead she frowned and her lips tightened. So it was a rather grim-faced pair who entered on Farwell's announcement.

It was immediately obvious to them both that all was not well in the Sayre household. Lady Freya moved at once to Lady Tulliver's side and bent to assist her into the sitting posture she seemed to be attempting to gain. The Duke's eyes went from the emotionally exhausted older woman to the resplendent figure of his host. One quick glance at his ravaged face was enough to sound the warning to a man of Dane's *nous*. The housekeeper took herself and the fluttering maids off at once, and Farwell, thankfully, closed the doors behind them and himself.

"What has happened?" asked the Duke quietly.

"My granddaughter has run away," said the Earl, tight-voiced.

*"The King!"* wailed Lady Tulliver.

"There is that," admitted the Duke, fighting to repress any sign of the intense satisfaction he felt at this eleventh-hour reprieve. "Now we must quickly contrive how we can all get out of this coil the silly chit has involved us in with some measure of credit."

Lady Freya cast him a quick warning glance, but the damage was done.

"My granddaughter is not a silly chit, My Lord Duke," the control the old man placed on his voice only served to emphasize his anger and contempt. "She is a sensitive young woman who has run away from a situation which you, sirrah, have rendered insupportable, with your ill-bred mockery and brazen disregard of the obligations of a gentleman."

It is safe to say that Osric Dane had never been spoken to thus in his whole life. His head flung up, and dark red color showed in his cheeks. How he might have replied to the Earl will never be known, however, since the butler, with a distinctly harassed expression, once more threw open the doors and announced six members of London's highest circle. The two gentlemen were compelled to present not only an air of complaisance, but a mutual regard which was, at the moment, the farthest thing from their desire. Indeed, observing their punctilious deference to one another, Freya's lips twitched in the first smile she had wished to give in two days.

The newcomers were of course aware that something very important was the *raison d'etre* for this dinner, and were, each according to his or her own nature, making coy or prying references to it, when Farwell appeared at the open doors yet again to announce "His Majesty, the King!"

At once all the ladies present curtsied deeply, and the gentlemen bowed.

"And where," demanded His Majesty jovially, "is the charming Belinda?"

# Chapter 5

The Duke felt the familiar lift of spirit which had always been his response to a challenge. Social disaster loomed over the old soldier beside him and the man's granddaughter— George IV was notoriously jealous of his dignity and had had to suffer so many slights during his Regency that he was quick to take offense even when none was intended. Almost without a pause after the King's question, Osric Dane stepped forward with a wide, mischievous smile on his well-cut lips.

"A word in your private ear, Your Majesty," he said, clearly enough so that all the polite yet avid auditors could hear him.

Majesty, pleasantly titillated, met the Duke's smile with one of his own. His eyes sparkled in anticipation. "What's to do, Osric?"

"My intended has—" the Duke paused provocatively, not daring to cast a glance at the rigid old soldier beside him, "—*caught the mumps*, Sire! We've removed her beyond the hazard of infecting *you*, of course!" He chuckled. "You must forgive the child! She really didn't *mean* to do it!"

Caught by surprise, the King began to chuckle, as much at Dane's expression of humorous dismay as at the information vouchsafed. The guests, relieved by royalty's amusement, joined the laughter heartily. The astounded Farwell, entering to announce dinner, was first startled and then comforted to observe a scene of universal merriment.

The King, with laughter still shaking his obese body, bent over to whisper a salted comment into Dane's ear. Then with the beautiful Lady Freya upon his arm, he led the way into the dining room. Farwell had already had the extra place setting removed. The King, well pleased with the elaborate decorations, and well aware of the toothsome and lavish meals prepared by the Earl's cook, was delighted with his table companions, the two most attractive women in the room. He settled his enormous bulk into a comfortable chair and prepared to enjoy a pleasant evening.

When all the company had been seated, and the footmen began to serve the luscious meal, the Duke cast a quick glance down the table at his host, and encountered so grim a look that he immediately felt his own temper ruffling, and began to wonder if anyone but himself could have snatched success from the jaws of disaster. For certainly the old boy hadn't had a word to say in response to the King's catastrophic question!

Feeling very superior, the Duke set himself to charm the King and the other guests, and succeeded so well that, when the ladies withdrew and the gentlemen sipped their brandy, the King was pleased to tell the Earl that he had never had a pleasanter dinner. The royal guest taking his departure half an hour later, the party broke up with enthusiastic congratulations to the Earl and Belinda's chaperone, Lady Tulliver, on a most enjoyable evening.

When all the guests but Osric Dane and his sister had departed, the Earl said in a grating voice, "Will you join me in my bookroom for a few minutes, My Lord Duke? I believe we have something to discuss."

The Duke's smile was icily civil. "I am sure you are right, sir."

At this point the Lady Freya surprised everyone by announcing, in a voice as cold as her brother's, that she believed the discussion should take place in the Gold Salon, with herself in attendance.

"For I shall take leave to inform you, sirs,

that I am as deeply involved as either of you in this matter, having acted as Belinda's sponsor into the *ton*, and having come to love the girl for her sweetness and merry spirit. I am convinced that neither of you is considering *her* feelings in the slightest."

This remark naturally pleased neither of the gentlemen, and sent Lady Tulliver into another of her spasms. Going to the bellpull, Lady Freya summoned Farwell and asked him to send Mrs. Munn to them at once. Then she bent over the weeping Lady Tulliver.

"You must permit Mrs. Munn to help you to your room, ma'am. I am sure your dresser will be able to give you a soothing posset to assist you to sleep. For it has been a—a demanding evening, has it not?"

Lady Tulliver, with a piteous glance at the two iron-faced gentlemen, was understood to agree, and the words "most considerate," "my wretched nerves," and "so alarmed for the poor child" were gasped out before Mrs. Munn entered to escort the poor lady from the room. At which point Freya cast a look of dislike at the two fuming gentlemen and said baldly, "Now let us discuss this miserable business without roundaboutation, if you please! You have made a fine mull of it between you, have you not?"

Both gentlemen received this thrust with every evidence of surprise and anger. Freya silenced their protests with a firm, "Be quiet!"

which shocked them into silence. Freya turned first to her host. "I must apologize for my brother's lack of tact in making no effort to heal the breach between himself and your granddaughter. In his defense it might be urged that he had no possible way of avoiding the King's summons the night of my ball, nor of removing himself from George's presence before being given leave to go, thus delaying his arrival until after Belinda had left. On the other hand, even granting the extreme provocation she endured from Dulcinia Wegg, it was childish of Belinda to have left the ball in such an obvious huff. You, sir, should have advised her so, and restrained such a show of pique as she presented."

"Hot-at-hand, was she?" sneered the Duke.

"Could you wonder at it, My Lord Duke, when the whole ballroom was abuzz with speculation as to your reasons for failing to show your front?" snapped the Earl. "And for one who vaunts himself as a past master in resolving difficult situations, you showed neither resource nor, indeed, common courtesy in dealing with Belinda. Likening her to a snake! Calling her a schoolroom chit! Making her a figure of fun in the *ton*—as you did again tonight!" The fierce eyes glared at the younger man from under beetling eyebrows.

"Have you finished?" the Duke said between closed teeth.

"He may have done so—I have not," said

45

Dane's sister. "Permit me to tell you that, while there are excuses for the General's folly, there are none for yours. I find your conduct reprehensible. After all, as we are so frequently reminded, your forte is diplomacy. A sixteen-year-old boy could have handled events more smoothly than you have done this past three days!"

At his glare of outrage, his sister began to enumerate coldly, "First, the night of my ball. You could surely, with all your *nous* and skill, have maneuvered that fat old fribble to release you early for my party! I suggest that you were taking out your own ill-humor upon your hostess and upon the unwelcome bride chosen for you."

Both men presented faces of horrified alarm at such unforgivable plain-speaking.

"Oh, let us have the gloves off," said Freya, wearily. "You owe it to a girl who has been so hurt she is fleeing from the only security she knows!"

"I must inform you, My Lady, that not only will I not insist upon the match, I will actively oppose it. My son must have been out of his mind when he wished for the connection!" snapped the Earl.

Before the affronted Duke could get his breath to reply to this insult, Freya had rattled in again. *"Second,"* she continued the attack upon her brother, "your smug complacence was so great that you made no effort to heal the hurt your ill-advised comments had dealt a young woman who might have expected at least common civility from her future husband! Did you call to offer your apologies? Did you send flowers or even a charming gift? No, you allowed pique or arrogance to dictate your actions. If this is the way you have behaved in the capitals of Europe, I cannot understand your reputation as a Nonpareil."

"I shall not listen to this fishwife's harangue!" the Duke ground out. "Lord James, I bid you good-night! Freya, do you accompany me, or may I send back the carriage for you?"

"I shall come with you, brother," said Freya. "My Lord, I pray you will permit me to call tomorrow to learn if you have had word from Belinda!"

"Good-night, Lady Freya," said the Earl in a voice from which all human warmth had departed.

With one lingering, anxious glance, the woman hurried after her brother. When he heard the outer door close behind them, the Earl strode over to the mantel and leaned his head upon his clasped hands on the cold marble. He stayed in that position for a long time.

\* \* \*

The brother and sister sat silently in the luxurious coach which carried them to the Lady Freya's house. Her brother, seething with fury at the attacks he had been subjected to, could not trust himself to speak. Freya was silent through fatigue and worry over the whereabouts of Belinda. Arriving at home, they dismounted and went in through the doors the butler was holding open for them. Freya halted in the hallway.

"Will you have a drink? Coffee?"

The Duke did not pause on his way to the great staircase. "Nothing, thank you," he said coldly.

"But we have to talk—to decide what to do about Belinda," protested Freya.

"I shall do nothing about her. You, of course, will act as you wish." He paused at the foot of the stairs, the light of many candles making his hair shine like new-minted gold. "I shall be leaving quite early in the morning. So this will be good-bye as well as good-night."

If he thought to bring her remorsefully to a sense of her own shortcomings, the Duke failed in his purpose. His sister straightened and glared at his handsome, irascible countenance.

"I have never been so little in charity with you as this minute, brother! Go, then! Run away like a petulant child from the mischief

48

you've made! But if anything happens to that girl because of you—!"

"It will not be my fault if an ill-behaved hoyden gets herself into a scrape!" snapped His Grace, furiously. Then, turning, he ran lightly up the stairs.

# Chapter 6

Osric Dane rode his stallion, Ben, away from his widowed sister's elegant London mansion very early the following morning. During a sleepless night he had penned a formal apology to the Earl for anything he might have said the previous evening which could have offended the old martinet. Couched in diplomatic language, it was calculated to soothe any but the most savage breast. He did not, however, so far abandon cautious self-interest as to make any promise of reparation, or seek an appointment to discuss any future development of the arranged marriage. In fact, it was His Grace's devout hope that the Earl would have had such a bellyful of that arrangement that he would wish never to hear mention of it again...thus allowing My Lord Duke to escape the trap in which he had so nearly been caught.

Himself a high stickler, Dane was aware that his conduct, while successful in preventing an open scandal, could perhaps have exposed the Earl's grandchild to the spiteful laughter of the ill-disposed. With a sardonic smile he recalled the pretty Wegg girl and her gawky friend hanging on his lips at Freya's ball when he took out his annoyance at the snare in which his father had ridiculously entangled him. He shook his head. *Conduct not up to your usual standards, my boy!* he chided himself. To speak disparagingly of any lady in public—what had he been thinking of? And then at the Earl's dinner party, had it been annoyance or relief he had felt on learning that the chit had run away rather than meet him? Although he still felt some resentment at the Earl's hostile reception of his efforts, he was coming to realize that his exercise in lightning diplomacy might have been considered to lack sensitivity and compassion.

It was so rarely that My Lord Duke experienced remorse over his own actions that he did not recognize the emotion, but as he left London behind him and directed Ben into the sweet-smelling countryside, he acknowledged an uncomfortable feeling. This discomfort fanned his anger against the chit who had precipitated the whole imbroglio. Since he had left his sister's home without requiring breakfast from her servants, he found the pangs of hunger exacerbating his ill-humor. By the time he decided to stop for a luncheon at a small inn, he was in a fury at the Earl, Freya, George IV, his own valet, his groom—both of the latter were actually blameless, since he had failed to notify them of his abrupt departure—and, above all, at Miss Belinda Sayre, the source and cause of all his discomfort.

His anger was not assuaged by the wretched service and deplorable cuisine at the hostelry of his choice. Over a greasy stew of unrecognizable meat and revolting vegetables, My Lord Duke felt his resolve hardening. This Belinda must be brought to a full acceptance of her own shortcomings in forcing a situation wherein a blameless, much put-upon gentleman was compelled to flee from the amenities of London and the company of his peers, rusticated like a naughty child in surroundings which offered him nothing but disgust. Rising abruptly from the dirty table, he summoned the host by the simple action of pounding upon the floor—also dirty—with the chair upon which he had been sitting.

The landlord came bustling in belligerently, but was soon reduced to a sense of his own inadequacies and those of his inn.

"Is Sayre Court in this vicinity?" snapped

the Duke. *Now why the devil did I ask that?* he wondered.

The landlord was compelled to admit a complete lack of knowledge of the residences of Peers of the Realm, local or otherwise, but offered to bring the angry gentleman another mug of beer. This was an unfortunate move, since it precipitated a deluge of criticism. Much chastened by this scathing denunciation of his house, his menu, his intelligence, and especially his beer, the wretched man finally managed to insert a word into the masterly flow of invective, and to suggest that his honor might wish to talk to Parson, who was a right knowledgeable old party, able to put any gentleman right.

This suggestion being received with revulsion, for a reason the landlord had no way of knowing, the fellow offered another. The stage from London stopped at Willowhill, a mere five miles up the road, and its driver would surely be able to tell him whether or not the residence he sought was on this particular highroad.

Not completely satisfied, but feeling a stagecoach driver to be preferable to a Parson at this juncture in his affairs, the Duke remounted his horse and set off briskly along the highroad, to the relief of the innkeeper.

In Willowhill, Dane struck it lucky. There were three inns, all of them a great many cuts above the miserable den in which he had

had his stomach insulted earlier. He was able to get a glass of choice brandy, probably smuggled, and being somewhat mellowed by the glow it induced, His Grace fell into conversation with a pleasant-faced, well-dressed man who was also playing off his dust. Upon inquiry, this gentleman admitted to a fair knowledge of the great houses in the county, and was able to announce that the Earl of Sayre's principal seat was not located anywhere in the neighborhood, but he rather thought he had heard of a Sayre Court belonging to the Earl in Devonshire.

This matter disposed of, the gentleman introduced himself as Eugene Newell, baronet, and My Lord Duke felt compelled to announce himself, for no reason he could immediately identify, as Peregrine Random.

"Ah!" his companion nodded with commiseration, quite mistaking the look of embarrassment on the other man's features. "M'cousin's in the same boat. Mother a romantic. Named the boy Parsifal Galahad. Father died before he was born, or she wouldn't have gotten away with it. Minute he came came of age, poor devil bought his colors and hasn't been home since. Believe he managed to conceal his given names when enlisting. Told 'em his initials stood for Peter George. His Colonel knows, but respects the lad's privacy."

Dane shared his laughter, but with only a

part of his attention. The other part was belatedly considering his conduct of the morning. To rush off in a huff from Freya's house was, he felt, so unlike his usual style that it merited a close scrutiny. And why the deuce was he inquiring about the country residence of the Earl? It came upon him like a thunderbolt that he had, somewhere in his mind, taken it upon himself to seek out the maddening little chit who had so threatened his comfortable image of himself, and make sure she was safely bestowed. He frowned thunderously.

His new-met companion was regarding him with some alarm. "I say, Random, no offense meant, you know! Peregrine is not such a bad name, after all! Only think if you had been called Parsifal Galahad—or Ulysses Gamaliel—or, uh, Waiting-for-the-Light—!"

A reluctant grin broke over Dane's face. "You made that one up!"

"On my word, fact! Good friend of my father's is a Quaker. Called his son that. Everyone's shortened it to Wait. Boy doesn't seem to mind."

On the strength of shared laughter, the two young gentlemen had a second brandy, and then the Duke, feeling much restored, took leave of his companion amid mutual expressions of goodwill.

The rest of the day passed swiftly, and the Duke was able to rack up at a tolerable inn that evening. For some reason, his spirits were much lighter as he set out, well rested and well fed, the following morning. He decided that the source of his improved temper was his conviction that the chit would surely have retired to her grandfather's principal seat when she wished to avoid having to face the laughter of the *ton*. Where else indeed would she go? A child of eighteen, with no skills fitting her for employment, and probably no wish to bestir herself over anything but her coiffure and her wardrobe, would seek the secure haven of her childhood home.

Having settled this to his satisfaction, and being much impressed by his own patience, forgiving nature, and generosity in seeking the girl out, the Duke was suddenly struck by a disagreeable thought. When he found her, what would he do with her? He debated this question in his mind for a long time, keeping Ben at a fast lope, and was only recalled to a sense of his surroundings by the increasingly restive behavior of his battle-trained mount. He focused his gaze and scanned the terrain. Just a little ahead of him, the Duke perceived a line of gypsy caravans, with a mounted escort of colorfully dressed riders. One at least of these latter had become aware of the Duke's headlong approach, for he had dropped back a little and was waiting by the roadside, facing the advancing horseman. His Grace, while not particularly nervous, was reassured to know he had a loaded pistol in its holster on his saddle, as well as a couple of other weapons less obviously displayed.

"Give you good-day, sir!" said the big gypsy, with a wide but not particularly mirthful smile.

"Good-day to you, sir," responded the Duke, his own smile easy and open. "That's a fine animal you're riding."

A frown tightened the other's black brows.

On seeing it, the Duke laughed with real amusement. "No, I am not challenging your ownership of the beast. I do not ask embarrassing questions—nor do I answer any."

The scowl faded into rather a grim smile as the gypsy scrutinized the Duke's stallion. Then the black gaze moved over the well-tailored riding coat, the strong muscular body, and the arrogant face of the solitary rider. "You're not saying you've no right to the horse you ride?"

"Oh, Ben's mine. But it happens I've no wish to be explaining why I'm riding him on this particular road, nor where I am bound."

The gypsy smiled broadly. "You would have me believe you are leaving London for reasons more urgent than to escape your creditors? Did her husband come home too soon? Or are you running shy of a duel?" The bright black eyes mocked him.

"You've a deuced sharp tongue in your

head," said the Duke, no whit disconcerted by these jibes at his morals and his courage. "And from the sound of you, a gently trained one."

"Oh, aye, A'm eddicated," answered the gypsy in broad mimicry of a rustic lout.

"Can you present me to your chieftain?" asked the Duke, a sudden plan flashing into his mind.

The gypsy bowed, and one darkly tanned hand touched his chest. "You are addressing him, sir."

Dane took a long, assessing look at the gypsy. The man was, if anything, taller than himself, and possessed a brutal face and a strong, heavily muscled body. He was wearing a silky black shirt over a pair of buckskins, and his well-made riding boots had been recently polished. The horse he rode was a great savage beast and looked every whit as dangerous as its master.

"My name is Random," offered the Duke.

"I am Anton, called The Whip," answered the other, grinning slightly and touching the braided leather handle of a heavy whip which hung from his belt, its thong efficiently coiled for instant action.

Dane smiled, elevating one eyebrow. "'The Whip'?"

Almost before his eye could catch the motion, the gypsy had the stock in his hand and had sent the iron-tipped lash curling out to flick the top button from Dane's riding coat. So swift was the action that Ben had not time to rear or shy before the lash was back in The Whip's hand and he was coiling it neatly, his eyes never having left the Duke's face.

Dane had not flinched. He admitted wryly that he hadn't had time—the attack had been lightning fast and completely unexpected. "I'll never make that mistake again," he said. "You have me positively quaking in my boots!" and he laughed with genuine admiration.

The gypsy studied him. "So you say. Yet you do not appear to be afraid. Perhaps you are not the soft townsman that you look?"

"Oh, I'm as soft as any other man," Dane answered. "If you had aimed at my face rather than at my coat button, I'd be sporting a fine scar as a memento of our meeting."

The gypsy seemed unsatisfied. "And what would I be sporting?" His dark eyes flicked at the holstered pistol on Ben's saddle. "Are you a sharp at the pops?"

But the Duke was not giving his full attention to Anton. He had caught a sound almost below hearing level coming from behind him. The gypsy's eyes did not move from his face, but there was an awareness in their expression. The Duke had not been one of Wellington's hell-born babes for nothing. He touched Ben with an almost imperceptible gesture. The great stallion leaped from its standing position toward The Whip, bringing Dane's body so close to the gypsy's right arm that he could not lift his whip. At the same moment a small black pistol appeared in Dane's hand and was thrust against the gypsy's throat.

"Why, sir, if that bravo of yours who is lumbering up behind me comes one single step closer, my hand might shake so hard with fear that I would blow your head off— quite by accident, of course! I would regret it very much!"

He waited, entirely relaxed and at his ease, his big hand rock-steady, the small deadly weapon pressing lightly against the gypsy's neck. Ben, well trained as his master, stood like the very statue of a horse.

A grin of reluctant respect appeared on The Whip's face. "My men would make you regret it, be sure of that! But I'd be too dead to enjoy your pain," he said softly. Then raising his voice slightly, "Enough, Pablo! Quebracho— all of you—easy! This hidalgo has proved himself a match for a Rom, at least today!" Then, staring at the Duke, he demanded, "What would you with my people, Gorgio?"

"I would ride with you, and share your fire," said Dane, slipping the small pistol into its pocket in the turned-back cuff of his riding coat.

"To what purpose?" the gypsy leader persisted. "My folk have enough trouble from

you English without sheltering some rene-
gade and finding ourselves inside one of your
stinking jails."

"I will guarantee that that will not happen," said the Duke quietly. "I might even
help a little with the foraging—you do live
off the country in the main, do you not?"

"You were a soldier?" The Whip asked, ignoring the Duke's question. His glance took
in the other man's sober elegance.

"In the Peninsula," the Duke confirmed his
guess. "Where I judge your people have also
spent some time? When you called me *hidalgo*, your accent was pure Castilian."

In spite of himself Anton's cheeks reddened
slightly with pleasure. "We are Gitano," he
said shortly. "But the Romany chal is never
anchored to one spot. The wide world is his
demesne!"

There was a mutter of approval from the
men who rode near them.

The Duke met Anton's hard, bold glance.
"It suits me to ride down into Devon for a few
days, perhaps longer, but I've no wish to
trumpet my presence. I would give you my
parole that your band will come to no harm
through letting me accompany you, but I'm
damned sure you and your Roms are able to
handle anything the stupid Gorgios could try
against you!"

There was a chorus of pleased laughter
from the gypsies, who now drew their horses

in close order around the two men. The Duke showed no sign of discomfort, but when one youthful Rom deliberately let his horse jostle the stranger, His Grace gave Ben the office, and the great stallion reared and leaped backward, almost unseating the presumptuous youth. This defensive maneuver occasioned a good deal of mirth, and the boy, eyeing Ben and his rider warily, met the Duke's innocent smile with reluctant admiration.

The Whip led the way smartly now, riding past the five large, brightly painted caravans drawn by magnificent draft horses. The Duke did not try to converse at the faster pace The Whip had set. He noted, however, that the gypsy horsemen now formed an effective guard around the wagons. Dane, well aware of the jealous regard in which Spaniards held their womenfolk, did not permit himself to stare at the girls who were driving most of the vans, only observing that they handled the reins with skill, and that they were brightly dressed and well pleased with themselves and their activity. It seemed a happy and well-found band, and the Duke glanced at its leader with respect. He found Anton's black gaze full upon him.

"You are to be congratulated upon your providence, Anton," he said sincerely. "Your tribe is in excellent condition."

The Whip shrugged this aside. "Where exactly do you go?" he asked.

"Into Devon. I'll find my way from there."

"We go on to Cornwall," vouchsafed Anton. "I have connections there. They are Gorgio, but they do not scorn their Romany kin."

"Why should they, indeed?" the Duke said. "I'll wager you can trace ancestry back to India. You are a proud people."

"True." The Whip rode on in a brooding silence. Then abruptly he called for one of his men and galloped ahead of the caravans. The Duke thought it politic not to try to accompany him. Instead he maintained a steady canter. Within a few minutes he was joined by the gray-haired gypsy he had heard addressed as Quebracho. This oldster wore a black velvet coat of a cut not seen in England, and a black, flat-crowned hat with a wide brim. The Duke thought the costume had a most comfortable look, the hat especially being capable of deflecting the sun's rays from the eyes of a horseman. For a few moments the two men exchanged such desultory comments as are possible between men riding on horseback. Then His Grace had an idea. He had already made the sudden decision to accompany the tribe to Devon, so that his arrival in the Earl's home district would not be instantly observed and widely reported. After the unpleasantness of his late encounter with the Sayre family, he was far from eager to have the Earl learn that he had so quickly sought out his reluctant fiancée. But who would expect the Duke of Romsdale to be consorting with a gaggle of gypsies? Now he realized that he would be even less conspicuous if he were dressed like his traveling companions.

"Where could I purchase such a coat and hat as you are wearing, sir?" he asked. "They are handsome and suitable for travel."

The old man appeared pleased at the comment. "I am my nephew's—what you would call—quartermaster," he said with a smile. "In my van I have such garments as our men might need on a long journey. I shall be happy to let you make a choice." The keen old eyes scanned His Grace's wide shoulders and well-muscled frame.

"A hat like yours, especially, senor," the Duke urged with a smile.

"Why do you seek to become like us, I wonder?" the old fellow grinned. "Is it that you are tired of being a Gorgio and would seek to be a Romany Rye?"

The Duke gave his charming smile. "I've already figured that a Gorgio is an Englishman—"

"It is any man who is not Rom," corrected the oldster.

"—but what, pray, is a Romany Rye?" continued the Duke, smiling.

"That is a man who wishes to ride with us, speak our language, share our life," defined Quebracho.

"Are there many such?"

"A good few. And some of them we accept. Fewer women seek to follow the gypsy patteran, but there are some. The Whip's mother was one such. A self-willed daughter of good Gorgio family, who saw his father at a festival in Cornwall, where our Romany chals displayed their horsemanship. She left her home that night and came with us. I do not believe she ever regretted it. She taught her son all that she herself knew, and he learned well." The old man hesitated. "He is a very dangerous man, Rye. Do not underestimate him."

The Duke nodded sober agreement. "Believe me, I shall not, Quebracho! I have no plan which threatens anything the tribe possesses, only a very pressing need to go down into Devon without being recognized. Still, I thank you for the warning."

"If you have no secret plan, you have nothing to fear," said Quebracho quietly.

Dane felt uncomfortable as he considered his mission to survey the elusive Belinda Sayre. If the old gypsy noted his embarrassment, he did not comment.

Dane decided it was time to change the subject. "Does your name have a meaning, like The Whip's?"

Quebracho chuckled. "Verdad! It means axe-breaker. I am such a tough Rom that they would say the axe blade would shatter on my hide! My given name, Alphonso, has almost

66

been forgotten." He motioned to one of the larger vans being driven by a young man. "Come to my storehouse and let me get a hat for you, senor, for we ride into the westering sun."

By dusk, when The Whip gave the signal to make camp for the night, the Duke was more than ready to dismount and ease the ache in his muscles. He was impatient with himself, watching the lithe agility of the gypsy men as they dismounted, set the wagons in a semicircle, and led all the horses to a picket line. The Duke joined them, unsaddling Ben and rubbing him down. The old skills came back to him, in spite of the recent years during which he had unthinkingly turned his mounts over to his grooms. When he finally led Ben to the line and looked about him for fodder, he found Bracho at his shoulder, holding out a leathern feed bag full of grain. Gratefully the Duke strapped it over Ben's head.

"My thanks, Quebracho," he said softly. "When I settle with you for the clothing I hope to buy, I shall also contribute to the cost of feeding Ben and myself."

Bracho shrugged. "I did not doubt it. Now come to the fire and rest until food is ready. I promise you will enjoy it."

The Duke did indeed enjoy the spicy stew which was served to him as he joined the group of men around the fire. The Whip had chosen a clearing in a small wood near the highway as the night's campground, and the Duke, an old campaigner, was unable to fault him. The wood hid the encampment from the road, and the fire, although bright enough to provide light and some warmth, was well screened by the caravans as well as by trees and underbrush, and would not be noticed by a casual scrutiny from the highroad.

Lying back against his saddle with a satisfied groan, the Duke looked around him with pleasure. This was a good life, he decided. It had all the challenge and interest of a campaign without the inevitable death and suffering of war. The gypsies appeared to be a happy company—there was laughter, some horseplay among the younger men, and considerable good-natured jesting between the men and the women.

These latter were a strong, handsome group, carrying their heads proudly, dressed in gowns which accentuated their graceful bodies. Dark eyes shone and sparkled; red lips pouted and smiled. *Careful*, he warned himself. Let these fighting cocks think you are encroaching, and they'll have you drawn and quartered before you can say *"pax"*—or should it be *"paz"*?

At his shoulder he heard Bracho's voice. "If you will come with me, I'll fit you out in a costume which will help you to look like one of us—if you'll cover that guinea-gold hair!"

"Gracias," said the Duke. "I'll take one kerchief for my head. I see you wear one under your hat. It's a dashing style." The Duke got quickly to his feet and followed the old man to the largest of the wagons. After a very satisfactory ten minutes spent in making his choices from the garments Quebracho produced for his approval, he took out his heavy purse and insisted upon paying for the clothing.

"Do you wish a blanket, senor?"

"No, thank you. I'll just roll up in my coat and sleep by the fire. I often did so in the war. Good-night."

The old man shook his head. "You have much to learn of our ways, Gorgio. You should have bargained with me, not given me my first asking price! Ah, well! I did not charge you for the head scarf."

Chuckling, the Duke approached the fire. It was burning low. Someone was strumming gently on a guitar, and a pleasant baritone was softly crooning a love song. Light shone warmly through the curtained small windows of the caravans. It was a soothing lull after the stress and embarrassment of his experience in London. His Grace was pleased to commend his wisdom in taking matters into his own hands to settle the question of his arranged marriage. A few days in the country, wooing the little minx out of her sulks, then a triumphant return to the Metropolis with the girl gentled and adoring, malleable to his wishes. Or, if she proved to be quite unacceptable, it would surely be easy to discourage her to the point where she would gladly agree to end the archaic arrangement. He removed his boots, and, wrapping his coat around him, stretched out for the night with his head on his saddle.

# Chapter 7

When the Honorable Belinda Sayre took a
hired carriage to the Saracen's Head Inn to
catch any kind of west-traveling coach which
would get her away from the searing humiliation of the past three days, she had in mind
no more daring escapade than a flight to her
real home, the Earl's estate in Devonshire.
She had no wish to cause her grandfather
worry. Of course he would know where she
had gone and would seek her out in a few
days when his temper had cooled a little. He
would still be very angry, and there would be
a scene, perhaps several, but eventually
Grandy would accept the fact that this arranged marriage was an affront to himself as
well as to her, since *that man* so obviously did

not wish to join himself to the Earl's family. So she set her dainty jaw and kept tears from her eyes with a real effort, and occupied her mind sensibly during the trip with what story she would offer the staff at Sayre Court—all old friends, allies—and critics.

It then occurred to her, with a pang of fear, that the Earl might not be the only angry visitor to the Court. What if the Duke decided he *did* wish to marry her? Or, more likely, that he must honor his father's commitment, whatever his own feelings in the matter? A lowering thought! As the much-indulged only grandchild of the Earl of Sayre, Belinda had never known humiliation until now. Must she be wedded, willy-nilly, to the arrogant nobleman? The girl set her teeth in a gesture of rebellion, and glared, narrow-eyed, at a young farmer seated across from her in the stage-coach. Her fulminating look caused the poor fellow to wonder what he had said or done to make the beautiful young lady glower at him in that crabbed way.

Belinda, who was quite unaware of his presence, was mentally running over all the devastating things she would say to the Duke if he dared to show his front at Sayre Court. She finally tired of this bootless exercise and when the coach stopped at a posting house to change horses, got down to partake of a hasty meal. The young farmer descended thankfully, and the married couple who shared the

72

seat with Belinda, having reached their destination, got off also. However, an elderly priest, an earthy-smelling farmer, his buxom wife and three daughters got on in their places, which so crowded the coach that Belinda began to wish devoutly that she had planned to spend the nights at inns rather than going straight through to Sayre Village. The excitements of the day finally caught up with her and she fell asleep, so firmly wedged between the side of the coach and one of the stout daughters that the jolting progress of the vehicle became a cradle-rock.

Although shorter in actual hours than the Earl's usual leisurely progress to and from his estate, Belinda's unbroken journey home to Sayre Court seemed to the girl to stretch to nightmare lengths of discomfort, and it was with heartfelt relief that she began finally to discern familiar landmarks. When she dismounted from the coach at Sayre Village, she did not wait for her small handcase to be thrown off into the road, but ran directly into The Climbing Man Inn to greet Mrs. Appledore, the landlord's wife, and demand a gig to take her at once to Sayre Court. While Appledore himself hurried out to retrieve her case, his wife insisted on making the girl a cup of tea while Ned harnessed the gig to drive Miss Belinda home. There was such a welcoming warmth and bustle that the girl cried a little, causing the landlord's good lady to mutter darkly about the folly of sending young lambs to the cruel City.

This enthusiastic reception was tame compared to the welcome Belinda received at Sayre Court. Most of the servants had been there longer than Belinda. They remembered with often embarrassing devotion her earliest remarks, actions, and occasional tantrums. In no time at all the girl was installed as safely as though she had never left home five months earlier for the London Season. From answers Belinda made to the probing inquiries of her old nurse, it swiftly became common knowledge that Miss Bel was fleeing from a Man, and moreover, a Man the Earl had insisted that she marry! The youngest footman, who was a mere forty summers, was heard to say that he'd personally black the Blade's eye for him, if he came prowling about the Court. Mrs. Mayo, the stout and dignified housekeeper, was heard to threaten the Monster with a dire fate, not specified, if he so much as laid hand on Missy. It remained for Dittisham, the Earl's butler, to express the sentiments of the whole staff.

"If," uttered Mr. Dittisham, in intimidating accents, "any Town Beau or Loose-screw comes ogling and leering after Miss Bel, *I shall know what to do!*"

This was felt to be a most satisfactory resolution, and the staff awaited the next development in the drama with avid interest.

Belinda only knew that the comforting ranks of her champions had closed loyally about her, leaving her free to take thought of what her own attitude should be. Exhausted by the rigors of her flight, she had convinced herself that her tormentor would pursue her to her sanctuary and seek by force to ravish her away from her devoted partisans. But after a good night's rest amid familiar surroundings, reassured by the lavish affection of her besotted staff, her natural high spirits began to reassert themselves, and she devised a Plan. It would surely be good enough to deceive such a pompous, conventional creature as the Duke must be, she told herself. Summoning Dittisham and Mrs. Mayo to her, and sending a groom for Appledore, she laid her scheme before them.

"You are all to say, if you please, that Miss Belinda Sayre has not come home, and that you do not know where she may be, if she is not in London. You must manage to look anxious about me if His Grace becomes too pressing or seems to doubt your word. But I am sure he will be vastly relieved to know that I am not here, and will return to London posthaste!"

Dittisham did not seem convinced by this lighthearted assumption. In his experience, Town Beaux who pursued innocent maidens to their lonely country estates were not so easily fobbed off.

Mrs. Mayo expressed doubts of a different kind. "The villagers'll see you about, Miss Bel, unless you've a mind to keep within doors by day and night. And that Man would have only to ask—"

"No, no, for Appledore shall tell them all what our story is to be," said Belinda lightly. "They'll back me up."

Mrs. Mayo was not convinced. "There's a couple of old biddies in the village who'd jump at the chance to gossip to a fine gentleman," she said grimly.

Belinda was struck by another idea. "I have it! You shall all say that there's only one of the Sayre's poor relations staying here—Miss Belinda's cousin-german at the fourth re-move!" She twinkled impishly.

"And what is the name of this removed cousin, if I may be so bold as to inquire?" asked Mrs. Mayo repressively.

"Why—Prudence Oliphant!" Belinda re-called the name of an old retainer who had lingered on at the Court in Belinda's child-hood. "Be sure everyone tells him that Cousin Prudence has no money and no expectations. A sort of unpaid drudge."

Mrs. Mayo looked scandalized. "Your grandfather wouldn't allow anything like *that* at Sayre Court, Miss Bel! Most generous he was with Miss Oliphant, your blessed mamma's former governess, and not a cousin French *or* German! As for your cousin Amabel—twenty years he kept her here, with every observance and attention! Unpaid drudge, indeed!"

Belinda chuckled. "But how the deuce is His Grace to know what my grandfather allows? He can hardly be aware that any of us are alive, except myself, and he's never set eyes on me! He has spent ten years racketing about the Continent, where God knows what strange customs prevail! I'm sure you'll be able to put the confounded fellow off," she finished encouragingly, ignoring Mrs. Mayo's scandalized face at her language, so close an echo of the Earl's. To herself Belinda added, *Pray Heaven he doesn't accompany Grandy down here!* But from all she knew of her grandfather, his pride and his temper, she could not visualize him offering to share a coach with the arrogant, insulting, contemptuous Duke of Romsdale.

# Chapter 8

My Lord Duke was having an unexpectedly good time on the road. After the years of formal, restricted behavior in the diplomatic circles of the capitals of Europe, this casual journey through the springtime freshness of the English countryside was a delightful escape to the carefree youth he had never really known. He enjoyed the cheerful banter of the gypsies while not for a moment deluding himself that they had truly accepted him as one of themselves. He rode with them on sufferance, although Bracho seemed almost to have adopted him as an apprentice into the ways of the tribe. The old man taught him to read the patteran—the signs which one gypsy or a tribe leaves to show others of their kind where they have gone. Dane's years as a soldier stood him in good stead during the ride, since he was nearly as skilled as the gypsies in snaring a rabbit, shooting birds on the wing, or requisitioning fruit and vegetables from a farm without the farmer's knowledge or consent.

The Duke's well-practiced charm made him persona grata to the women of the tribe as well, but he was scrupulously careful never to overstep the mark beneath the dark, enigmatic gaze of the gypsy men. His manner, friendly yet aloof, seemed to pique the gypsies, and they kept testing him in unexpected ways.

"You puzzle my people," Bracho told the Duke one morning as they were standing side by side, saddling their horses for the day's ride.

The Duke raised an eyebrow.

Bracho grinned. "Yes, they don't know quite what to make of you. You pay our women the tribute of your admiration, yet you refrain from making advances which our men might resent."

Dane strapped his bag behind Ben's saddle. "I have had a little training in self-restraint," he acknowledged.

Bracho shook an admiring head. "Perhaps I should warn you..." he began, when there was an interruption. A tall, slender woman, her dark hair caught under a brilliant red silk kerchief, her shapely body flaunting a gaily patterned full skirt and tight blouse, strolled over to the horse line. She was carrying a saddle and harness. With a careless nod and smile at the two men, she began to saddle a beautiful mare. Almost without conscious thought Dane moved over beside her.

"May I do that for you, Rauni?"

The beautiful face turned toward the Duke, and the huge dark eyes regarded him challengingly. Then the girl nodded once, and stood back.

The Duke saddled the mare, testing the girth before he led the animal to her. He held out his cupped hands to assist her to mount, but she sprang up into the stirrup lightly without assistance. As she rode off she favored the Duke with a provocative smile.

Bracho was shaking his head ruefully. "Never say I didn't warn you," he grinned.

The Duke stared at the brown, wrinkled face. "About that lady?"

"She is The Whip's chosen," Bracho informed him. "Only she is a stubborn piece, and very conscious of her worth. She will not give him the answer he wants. None of our young men dare to court her, knowing the chief has his eye on her. Like all women, Lara wants to trouble the waters."

"Thank you for the warning," Dane said seriously.

The old man merely shrugged and smiled.

The Duke was riding with the rear guard behind the caravans that afternoon when The Whip dropped back and took his place beside him. "Lara tells me you saddled her mare for her this morning," the chief began.

"As I would do for any lady," agreed Dane quietly.

Anton considered that, his dark, flat gaze holding the Duke's eyes. At length he nodded once, sharply. "She is to be my woman," he said arrogantly. "When I am ready."

"You are to be congratulated," said the Duke.

Nothing more was said, but the Duke had an uneasy sense that The Whip's eyes were often on him, and that several of the other Romany chals kept him under unobtrusive surveillance. Instead of making him angry at The Whip, the situation only confirmed Dane's bitter resentment against women. Troublemakers! They had only to enter the scene to create discomfort, embarrassment, hostility! As witness his own affairs—was not all going smoothly until the wretched business of the arranged marriage? It did not strike the Duke that that situation, at least, was none of Belinda Sayre's making. He was more than ready to blame the girl for all the unpleasantness he had had to endure since he returned to London from Europe. And now the gypsy girl was out to make trouble. *Women!*

Musing thus morosely, the Duke followed

the caravans and eventually found them making camp rather earlier than usual.

"We are going out to collect some dinner," Bracho advised him as they tethered their horses side by side.

"I'll come with you," offered the Duke, eager for a diversion. The carefree life of the open road was wearing a little thin: hard earth for a mattress, his saddle for a pillow, and his coat for a blanket; no hot water for shaving, and linen he had to clean by washing in whatever wretched creek or muddy pond might lie adjacent to the night's camping place. The Duke was forced to accept the fact that he was no longer eighteen and careless of comfort. But if he might get a little sport, it would relieve the boredom of the simple life.

Quebracho was shaking his head. "Better not," he advised. "The Whip is in a foul humor. You might get accidentally shot." He grinned at Dane's startled expression.

"Does he dare to leave me alone in camp with the beautiful Lara?" queried the Duke wryly.

"Oh, all the old women have been warned to keep an eye on you," advised the old man.

"Of the two choices, I'd prefer the men's guns," said Dane, more than half-serious.

"You begin to show wisdom," chuckled Bracho, walking toward the forest.

While the women made the fires and set

the great iron hooks deep into the ground beside them, ready for the cooking pots, the Duke sat by himself under a spreading tree at a little remove from the camp. The late afternoon sun was westering through the trees, filling the air with a golden haze. Suddenly a new quality about the low-voiced murmurings of the women struck the Duke's ear, and he was alerted to a change in the situation. He became aware of two men, dressed in the gaiters of gamekeepers, coming cautiously along the lane the caravans had followed to get to this clearing. Each man had a shotgun unobtrusively ready over one arm. They were peering cautiously around the encampment, trying to discover its strength before they announced their presence.

One of the older women came forward to meet them, asking them civilly enough what they wished.

"Where's all the Roms, Mother?" asked one of the keepers, while the other, gun at the ready, was busy scanning the environs.

"Gone to the village to buy food," said the woman, smiling toothlessly.

"That'll be the day," answered the gamekeeper. "Come on, old woman, we know they're poaching in milord's woods! You'd better start packin' yer gear. If yer not out o' here in an hour, we've orders to set fire to yer wagons."

"We have always had permission to stay

one night in Lord Denison's woods," retorted the old woman.

"That was the old lord," sneered the keeper. "He's dead this six months, an' his nevvie's given orders we're to roust you out. Seems he can't abide dirty, stinkin' gypsies!" the man laughed loudly.

His companion had discovered the Duke, seated under the drooping branches of the huge tree. He stepped closer to his fellow and said something under his breath. The first keeper swung quickly around and raised the shotgun.

The Duke, sprawled very much at his ease, raised an arrogant eyebrow.

"Wot're *you* doin' over there?" snarled the keeper.

"Waiting for my supper," replied the Duke calmly.

"There ain't gonna be no supper for the likes o' you! Help the woman to break camp!"

Beyond the clearing, a hint of movement caught the Duke's eye. He thought he recognized the brown velvet. He got lazily to his feet. "We are not going to break camp," he announced. "I have decided I like it here."

"'Tain't what you likes as makes any difference," the keeper advised him, his face turning brick red under the amused glances of the women. He made a threatening gesture with the shotgun. "Move, gallow's-bait, or I'll pepper yer hide wi' this!"

The Duke's head lifted contemptuously. In a sharp voice he said, "This nonsense has gone far enough! I see I shall have to inform you rustics of my name and style—although I had intended to wait until after dark to visit your master and make myself known. I am Major Romsdale of His Majesty's Fifty-Second. I am on special assignment to this area."

This statement made both gamekeepers laugh heartily, and their eyes flicked scornfully over the short green velvet coat and the stained buckskins. "That's a large one, that is! You ain't gonna gammon us yer with the *Preventives*—"

There was a sudden, arrested quiet among the listening women at the name of that hated group. Ignoring this, the Duke drew himself up into the unmistakable stance of a seasoned officer. "No, I am not, clod-pole! I am representing His Majesty on a secret mission which has nothing to do with the petty smuggling which takes place in this area—supported, as I am well aware, by the local petty aristocracy!" He interrupted himself, sure at last of the identity of the lurker at the edge of the woods. "Sergeant Axebreak!" he snapped. "Front and center!"

*"Sir!"* Quebracho snapped back, his military response secretly tickling the Duke's risibilities.

The old gypsy, delighted to take part in any charade which purported to fool the Gorgios, marched into the clearing with a fine pseudomilitary bearing. He halted in front of the Duke, quite ignoring the gamekeepers, and saluted smartly.

"Sir?"

"Have the scouts reported back to you?" barked the Duke, very much the Major of Dragoons.

"No, sir."

"Very well, then, resume your position." As the old man marched back toward the wood, the Duke faced the frowning keepers. "Now I shall tell you this *once only*. There is a notorious traitor who is seeking to escape from England. He is reported in this area, and is thought to be negotiating with smugglers for his passage to France. I shall not call on you as loyal Englishmen for aid against this traitor, for I have no confidence whatever in your ability to be of any assistance to me!" This was said with such a glare that the keepers found themselves trying to make excuses for their own inadequacies. The terrible Major appearing to be a little appeased, the head keeper ventured to ask if his honor wished to send a message to Lord Denison.

"Can we trust his loyalty?" challenged the Major.

"Oh, yes sir, indeed his lordship is as loyal as any man hereabouts!" avowed one keeper, while the other hastened to agree that there wasn't a loyaler man in these parts.

Their statements did not seem to impress the officer overmuch. "In that case, I will send no message. We shall do what we came for and be gone before daylight tomorrow. See to it that we are not disturbed!" he ended with such a fierce glare that the gamekeepers nearly fell over their own feet getting away from the spot.

There was a pregnant silence until the two intruders were well out of sight. Then the women drew closer to the Duke and stood in an admiring semicircle before him, smiling and talking softly. Quebracho loped silently into the glade, his grin a white slash in the dark face.

"No Rom could have done it better," he said with admiration. "The Whip and the others are in the woods, awaiting the outcome of your *engaño*, your trick. We like it very well!" he added, chuckling.

The Duke sensed new acceptance from most of the tribe as they sat around the fire later, enjoying Lord Denison's rabbits and birds. Only The Whip stayed aloof, his black gaze moving from the Duke's face to that of Lara, who had seated herself beside the hero of the hour. Finally becoming uncomfortable at the proximity, the Duke arose and made his way to where the chief sat.

"I told them we would be out of here by daylight," he began.

Anton shrugged. "That is well. Our business will be done by then." He stared hard at Dane. "Preventives?" he asked softly.

"Nay, I'm on a romantic errand," denied the Duke, and then cursed himself at the quick, hard set of the chief's body. "I am grateful for your hospitality," he hastened to say, "but I must leave you as soon as we get to Sayre, where my business is waiting."

"That should be about noon, the day after tomorrow," The Whip advised him. After a pause, he continued grudgingly, "Yours was a good ruse. We Roms enjoy a hoax well played. But I do not like you, Gorgio."

"I am your guest," the Duke reminded him. "It would hardly be seemly of me to tell you the feeling is mutual."

A reluctant grin tugged at the gypsy's hard mouth. "Yet you have managed to do so without being insulting. I begin to fear you, Gorgio."

"As I have always feared you," said the Duke.

"It seems we both know how to lie," retorted The Whip, for the first time that evening smiling easily.

The Duke let him have the last word. It was good diplomacy.

At noon of the second day after this encounter, the colorful procession of caravans wended its way down the Devon roads toward the sea. Ahead of them was a wood, stretching for a great distance on either side of the high-way. Running off toward the ocean on the left, enclosing this side of the forest, was a high stone wall.

Bracho, riding beside the Duke, pointed out the imposing barrier. "That is the boundary of Sayre Court," he said. "It is your destination?"

"I have some small business in the area," admitted the Duke. He had no fear that the gypsy would betray him to any Gorgio, but he was not ready to discuss his private affairs with anyone at this juncture.

The old man forbore to question him further, and the two rode in companionable silence. As the massive wall loomed nearer, Dane asked, "Shall you be staying in this neighborhood long?"

"Perhaps awhile," admitted Bracho. "The Whip has a friend here, and we have trading to do before we go to Cornwall."

Now the leading riders and the vans were entering the wood. The Duke noticed that the great stone wall also fronted the highroad at this point, and that the forest was giving way to ordered rows of fruit trees. A flash of movement from the top of the wall caught Dane's attention. A girl was perched on the old stone coping, her lovely, long bare legs dangling beneath a sober gray gown. On her small feet were sturdy black slippers, with which she was kicking idly at the wall. Her head was neatly covered with an old-fashioned mobcap, and her vivid little face, regrettably smeared with the juice of the fruit she was munching like any urchin, was turned to view the procession which approached her.

The Duke thought she was the loveliest girl he had ever seen.

For her part, Belinda was busily taking in the fascinating details of the cavalcade which was approaching her vantage point. First came several young men mounted on horses as fine as Belinda had ever seen. The men were dressed in brightly colored shirts with dark trousers and hats set rakishly on coarse black hair. Only as they came closer did the girl perceive that the colorful clothing was well worn, occasionally ragged, and that the hats, though gallantly cocked, were sometimes old and battered. The harnesses of the horses, however, gleamed with many brass ornaments polished to a glittering shine. The young riders were very much aware of the girl on the wall. Teeth gleamed white against swarthy skin as they smiled cheerfully at her.

The riders were closely followed by a line of large, covered vans or wagons, garishly decorated with red, yellow, and blue painted wooden scrolls and fretwork. Drawing each of these small houses-on-wheels was a magnificent draft horse expertly driven by a youth or a woman. Several spare horses were tied to the rear of the wagons. Bringing up the rear of this parade was a group of four horsemen, and it was upon the last two of these that Belinda's admiring glance rested longest.

They were worth looking at. Where the other gypsies, their gaily colored garments in various stages of picturesque disarray, resembled nothing so much as a flock of bedraggled parrots, these two riders wore an air of raffish elegance. The larger man wore a short, black leather vest over a red shirt, black leather breeches, and high boots. Around the thick column of his neck was a yellow kerchief. His coarse black hair was partly covered by a black felt hat, from under the broad brim of which his dark eyes glittered at the girl. From one earlobe dangled a gold ring. He did not smile, but he gave some signal to his stallion so that the great beast curvetted and danced a few steps as he moved past Belinda.

Greatly entertained, the girl transferred her delighted gaze to the other man. While not so huge as his companion, this fellow was big and well built. A pair of stained tight buckskins was molded to his muscular thighs, and a bright green velvet jacket stretched tight across broad shoulders. He stared back at the girl on the wall boldly, his eyes curiously intent.

At this moment several of the village dogs,

scenting an invasion, came racing down the road toward the gypsy caravans, barking furiously at the horses' hooves and at the wheels of the wagons. The gypsies called out taunts and jeers, rousing the self-appointed guardians to a frenzy. The girl on the wall joined the laughter, then, an impish smile lighting up her countenance, began to chant:

"Hark, hark, the dogs do bark!
The gypsies are coming to town.
Some in rags, and some in tags—"

Her laughing eyes took mocking notice of the Duke's velvet jacket—

"And one in a velvet gown!"

The Duke, who had never refused a fence or a challenge in his life, brought Ben onto the grassy verge between the highroad and the stone wall with a smooth, frightening rush. Reining in just below the small black boots, he doffed his newly acquired sombrero with all the grace of a Spanish caballero. Smiling up into the girl's startled face, he said softly, "Thank you for the welcome, little one! Shall I come up, or will you come down to me?"

This was taking the attack to the challenger indeed. The girl's cheeks blazed with color and her big brown eyes went wide.

The Duke grinned mockingly. "Is there not another verse, pretty one? Or are you already regretting the invitation?"

"It was not—I did not—" stammered Belinda, automatically smoothing down the gray skirts over her long, shapely legs.

"Too late," sighed the Duke, ogling them outrageously.

Well aware of the direction of the man's impudent stare, Belinda's lips tightened with anger. "You are insolent, sirrah!" she snapped, every inch the General's granddaughter.

"To accept the overtures of a beautiful girl?" the Duke teased. "Or did you think your position high on your master's wall would protect you from the gypsy's crude advances?"

Since this, in effect, was exactly what Belinda had thought, she was momentarily at a loss. Only momentarily, however. This boldly smiling man was a very different kind of male creature from the elegant young gentlemen who had paid court to the Season's newest Beauty. One could not be sure this fellow would respect the accepted boundaries of polite dalliance, if indeed he was even aware of them. Another look at the audacious gray eyes, shining with unholy amusement, told her she had better go warily with this one.

So, being Belinda, she ignored caution and struck out boldly. "Who needs protection from a mouse?" the General's granddaughter laughed scornfully.

To the Duke's affronted ears came a loud echo of the chit's mocking laughter as The Whip appeared beside him on the grassy verge.

"Not so successful with this one, Gorgio?" prodded Anton. He turned to the girl and swept off his hat, smiling seductively. "Pretty lady, there have been changes since last we came this way. Can you tell a poor wandering man if the Earl's writ still runs in this place?"

The girl got his meaning. "Sayre Home Wood is still a safe haven for your people," she acknowledged. "The Earl and his family are not in residence, but his bailiff will do business with you."

With a tiny smile at The Whip and no glance whatever at the Duke, the girl swung lithely around and vanished from the top of the wall.

The Whip laughed softly.

# Chapter 9

Belinda made her way up to the great house smiling complacently. It had done her good to put that presumptuous gypsy in his place. The insolence of him, trying to flirt with her! (If that was what his breathtaking advance had meant.) For a moment her heart had seemed to be in her throat, and the whole world to be restricted to a pair of challenging gray eyes, with a light in them she had never seen in a man's glance before.

*Gray?* Was not that an unusual color for a gypsy's eyes? The impudent creature had had a green silk kerchief about his head under the broad-brimmed hat, so that she had not been able to see the color of his hair. He hadn't worn an earring, either, as the big dark one did. At least *that* one had behaved with decent respect, his night-black eyes modestly hooded in his swarthy face.

Belinda sighed. They were fascinating, the gypsies. She had been aware from her childhood of their seasonal visits to Sayre Wood, although she had never been permitted to play with the laughing, dark children, or to visit their encampment. She knew that the traveling-folk brought Spanish wines and French brandies to the Earl, and that he was pleased to deal with them rather than "those rascally vintners in London."

Entering the house by the back door, she encountered Mrs. Mayo. The housekeeper immediately subjected her to a lecture on the shocking lack of decorum evidenced by her appearance in public so inappropriately costumed.

"*Bare legs,* Miss Bel! And wherever did you find that dress? In a ragbag, I'll be bound! What your grandfather would say, I do not dare to think! And your fine friends in London, too. Shocked they would be! When is this silly masquerade to come to an end, is what I wish to know?"

"After the Duke of Romsdale returns to the City we can be comfortable again, dear Mayo," coaxed the girl.

"But he hasn't even *come* yet, Miss Bel, and it's my belief that a great man like that would have better things to do with his time than to come chasing into the country after a girl he doesn't even like!" replied Mrs. Mayo, in the mistaken idea that she was offering comfort.

Since, however, her estimate of the situation marched too closely with Belinda's own, the effect was to depress the girl further. The idea had been growing in her mind that she might have been overestimating her own appeal in considering that so top-lofty a personage as His Grace the Duke of Romsdale would come running into Devon after a silly minx who had no more *nous* than to insult her Sovereign. He had given no indication that he wished to further his acquaintance with her—rather the contrary. It was a lowering thought. Worse, it brought with it the fear that her grandfather might have suffered a royal snub because of her intransigency. But in that case would the Earl not have repaired at once to Sayre Court, there to wait some sign of Majesty's forgiveness? She frowned. Whatever she did seemed to be wrong since this wretched Duke had returned to London from the capitals of Europe! If only he had stayed there, she might have been comfortable! Instead of which she was self-banished from the scene of her first social triumph, her whole future was shadowed, she was bored to distraction, and, ultimate disaster, forced to admit that the despicable Dulcinia had triumphed over her! A single tear overflowed from her eyelid and found its way down one cheek.

Mrs. Mayo observed this unusual reaction with alarm. What had she said to throw her darling into the dismals? That the Duke didn't like her? But the child had claimed from the start that *she* disliked *him!* Could it be—? Folding Belinda to her motherly bosom she crooned gently, "There, there, Miss Bel! It will all come out right! I've no doubt his lordship will bring the Man here if you want him, my dearie."

But Belinda had seen the light. "He will never come! I have given him such a disgust of me that he will probably cut me dead if he meets me in the street!" And even if he doesn't, her guilty conscience reminded her, he will utter more of his hateful witticisms, and reveal my folly, and all the *ton* will be sneering at my childish behavior. I should have stayed in London to face it out, not run like a scalded cat!

In an effort to get her mind off these depressing conclusions, Belinda said with forced brightness, "Dear Mayo, the gypsies are back! Will Hawkins be purchasing wines from them again this year?"

"The Earl's bailiff will do what is right and proper," said Mrs. Mayo, whose ethical position was the prevailing local one with regard to Free Trade. "Now do go up to your room, Miss Bel, and get out of that absurd costume!

Cook has your favorite scones for tea, and a trifle with cream and fresh berries."

Somewhat cheered by this intelligence, Belinda went up to her luxurious suite to wash her face and hands and don garments more suitable to her station. During the delectable repast she subsequently indulged in, she made firm resolutions to conduct herself with more propriety—for even a poor relation, she told herself, would hardly perch on a wall eating peaches, and exchange insults with gypsies! But it had been exciting, especially when that insolent creature had practically charged the wall. As though she were manning the redoubt of a besieged castle, and he the besieger! Ridiculous man, with that green silk kerchief over his hair under the foreign hat! Probably only too well aware of the romantic figure he cut!

The swarthy one might turn out to be what Grandy was wont to call *an ugly customer,* for all his meek demeanor and his absurd gold earring. He had not been displeased when she depressed the pretensions of his companion. He had been laughing as she left them. Well, it would serve his saucy friend right. Of course, Belinda would never see any of them again, she told herself virtuously. She might have made no attempt to do so, either, in spite of the boredom which was making her, to quote Mrs. Mayo, as cross as crabs, had not Fate intervened in the person of Dittisham.

That portly patriarch, strongly aware of his duty to the House, saw fit to comment upon the situation. As he was serving Belinda's solitary dinner that evening in the great shadowy dining room, he said, wistfully, "We shall go on better when his lordship returns to us, shall we not, Miss Bel?"

Belinda, while considering that viewpoint more than a trifle optimistic, knew what was expected of her. She nodded, and smiled up at the elderly servant.

Encouraged by this charming agreement, Dittisham continued, with the outspoken privilege of an old retainer, "In the meantime, Miss Bel, you must not attempt to go near the Home Woods while those gypsies are encamped there."

The girl peeped up at him through her long eyelashes. "Must I not, Dittisham?"

"*Miss Bel!* You know your grandfather has never permitted it! And especially not *now*, when the situation is...is delicate."

All traces of the playful smile vanished from the girl's face, and her brows drew together. "The situation—?"

Dittisham, unaware that her successful London Season had made changes in the child he had known all her life, rushed in where angels might have hesitated.

"I've had a note from his lordship, Miss Bel. He is not best pleased, I gathered, by what—

er—occurred in London before you left. He has instructed me and Mrs. Mayo to keep a— that is, to watch carefully over you until he comes."

Belinda set her teeth. Aside from the daunting fact that her grandfather had seen fit to communicate with Dittisham rather than herself, she was well aware that she was being justly rebuked for her want of conduct. Too proud to ask exactly what the Earl had told Dittisham, she was guiltily conscious that none of it could reflect credit upon herself.

"Keep a sharp eye upon the chit," was probably the kindest thing the old stickler had said. For one of the few times in her much-indulged life, she had been sharply and publicly reprimanded, and the fact that the reproof was well merited did nothing to soften the blow.

A few months previously, before what she was now compelled to regard as the ending of her successful come-out, Belinda would have accepted the Earl's strictures with chagrin, perhaps, but without resentment. Her honesty and habitual good humor would shortly have led her to make the necessary apology and restore the *status quo ante*. But now resentment dulled remorse, and the girl felt that she had been unjustly treated by those whose business it should have been to protect and defend her. So she summoned up a rather glittering little smile and said gently, "I'll keep your advice in mind, Dittisham."

# Chapter 10

The Duke was finding his alfresco existence very much to his taste—now that it was nearly over. With the assurance of clean sheets, a good mattress, and abundant hot water at his disposal by the next day, he was free to enjoy the delights of living with Nature...briefly. When the gypsies made their encampment in the Earl of Sayre's Home Woods, he lent a hand with the rest, unharnessing the majestic draft horses from the wagons and leading them to the line, then rubbing down and feeding them. Later he joined the youths who were pegging out the black tents in which the men slept who had neither wife nor caravan.

"Bachelor Officers' Quarters," he thought,

pleased that he would not have to spend another night under the stars, wrapped only in his greatcoat. That fashionable accoutrement was becoming lamentably stained by the rough usage he was giving it and was at best an inadequate covering against the heavy night dews. The Duke shook his head ruefully. He had lived soft for ten years and had lost the knack of adjusting to the rigors of campaign.

At this moment the beautiful Lara came to him bearing a full plate of the savory stew the older women had prepared in the great iron kettles. As he inhaled the appetizing steam, he admitted that this had been no rigorous campaign but a superb holiday from responsibilty. But now it was time to report back for duty. The first thing tomorrow morning, he would ride Ben to the inn with the odd name—The Climbing Man—and reserve their best room for a week. If he paid in advance, his guineas would weigh heavier than his raffish appearance. He would write to Freya, to the Ministry, and to Pliss, his valet, still waiting for him at Freya's home in London. He would direct that his groom bring Pliss and suitable clothing to him at once in his curricle. He sighed. If the letter was put on the Mail coach tomorrow, his holiday would be over in a few days. Decently clothed, he could pay a visit to Sayre Court and discover whether the Earl's granddaughter was in residence. If she were not, he had better get back to London without further delay and mend his fences. Already he was deeply regretting the petulance which had led him to place the girl in an equivocal position. Had it been petulance—or some deeply buried reluctance to give up his freedom? Freya was right, he admitted at last. He had behaved very badly indeed to the Sayres, and would probably have to eat a large serving of humble pie before the old martinet forgave him. The thought of having to placate a sullen—or worse, hysterical—eighteen-year-old bride filled him with dismay, but he would honor his father's word and marry her. Freya had seemed to think the girl had character, though her action in running away had not demonstrated it. Still, something might be made of her with time and careful handling. After all, he had brought much weightier problems to a successful conclusion.

He was roused from these gloomy thoughts by an awareness that the gypsy girl Lara was lingering near him, staring at him as he ate. Warning bells rang their tocsins in his mind. Devil take the wench! She would force him into a confrontation with The Whip if she kept up this behavior! He gave her a warning frown.

Lara's response was to sidle close to him and favor him with a provocative wiggle which set him grinning involuntarily. Little minx! Playful as a young tigress—and just as dangerous. *Careful!* he reminded himself, suddenly conscious of the attention this by-play was getting from the circle of gypsies eating around the fire. This was The Whip's girl; Bracho had warned him. He said softly, "Do you enjoy playing with fire, Lara?"

The girl shrugged and tossed her long, dark hair.

"Lara plays where she wishes. Lara belongs to no man, Gorgio! Lara will choose who is to receive her favors."

This speech was delivered in a tone loud enough to be heard—and easily misunderstood—by a jealous man. *Women!* thought the Duke. *A man's damned if he does and damned if he doesn't!*

The Whip rose from his stool by the fire. Throwing down his plate, he strode toward Lara and the Duke. Oh, well, thought Dane, I intended to leave the tribe tomorrow morning anyway. The gypsying had been a pleasure, and he was reluctant to end it with a fight.

The Whip loomed over him. Ignoring Lara completely, he said harshly, "What is it that you are telling my *chai*, Gorgio?"

Lara turned a wide, pleased smile on the chief, then a smug little grin on the Gorgio, obviously waiting for him to defy Anton. Oh, yes! thought the Duke, you'd enjoy seeing us at each other's throats, wouldn't you? Placing his plate of food carefully on the ground, Dane got to his feet to face the bigger man. He met the flat black gaze steadily.

"I was telling her that my father had pledged with his best friend that their children would marry. It is so sometimes with your people, is it not?" Without waiting for a reply, Dane continued, "I am traveling to meet my future wife now, to arrange the details of our wedding. Your fiancée said that, for her part, she would prefer to choose her own husband."

Not very chivalrous, the Duke decided, but serve the little troublemaker right! Fitted in with the speech she'd made about choosing who was to receive her favors—and every word of it true, he congratulated himself. Diplomacy!

Turning swiftly on the gaping Lara, The Whip caught her by the shoulder. "My patience is at an end! Speak now, or I shall choose another *chai* to be my queen," he told her in a most unloverlike voice.

"You would not!" she glared at him. "It is me you want—me alone!"

The chief's smile was as cold as his eyes. "Who are you to say what The Whip wants?" He released her shoulder, pushing her away from him, so that she staggered and almost fell. "I want a loving woman in my bed, not a peevish child!"

The Duke regarded Anton with admiration. He was tempted to cheer him on. But the girl was looking, wide-eyed, at the big gypsy.

"I am the prettiest woman in the tribe! You told me you would have none but the best!"

The Whip's glance flicked her contemptuously. "There are other tribes. And when we reach Cornwall, there are many pretty *didakis*—even Cornish girls—who might please me as well as you, or better."

The men, women, even the children around the fire were so still that Lara's gasp was plainly audible. "Didakis? You would take a half-breed to wife? Or a Gorgio mort? You—the chief?"

"Pral Veshengro's tribe is meeting us near Penzance," The Whip informed her. "He has a lineage as pure as any of ours—and he has two beautiful daughters, so I am told."

Lara stared up at him, the anger seeping from her face. A quick glance around the circle made her aware that every member of the tribe had heard what had been said. Her eyes returned to that swarthy implacable face. At last she bowed her dark head.

"Yes."

Anton waited, motionless.

Lara flung herself at him, beating on his massive chest. "Yes, I will be your woman—you devil!" she cried.

The Whip grunted and caught her to him with one hard arm.

"I accept your offer," he said with a triumphant laugh.

Everyone around the campfire joined in his laughter, the Duke very heartily indeed—and with considerable relief. He picked up his plate and walked around the fire, handing it with a word of thanks to the old woman who presided over the iron kettle. Then with a wave and a general "good-night," he walked over to the place where he had left his saddle and coat and lay down. He failed to notice the venomous glare Lara directed after his retreating form. Sleep came to him almost at once.

He awoke very early and left the tent to walk over to the stream which served as a lavatory for the gypsies. Washing his hands and face, he donned, for the last time, the raw silk shirt he had bought from Quebracho. He had rinsed it out himself at various streams and muddy ponds along the way, but its grubby condition had suddenly become offensive to him, in view of the fresh linen he would soon be wearing. So much for the joys of the open road, the Duke shrugged wryly.

He was fastening the buttons when he became aware of a stealthy noise in the underbrush near him. Someone was creeping close and making an effort to disguise his approach. Sudden visions of an ambush by the affronted Whip or by an ambitious youngling eager to test the Gorgio flashed in his head.

111

He was weaponless; his gun and stiletto were in their sheaths in his greatcoat. He finished buttoning the silk shirt, then casually bent to pick up the handkerchief he had used as a towel. With it, he palmed a large, jagged stone. Thus armed, he turned to face the inept attacker.

The sounds in the underbrush had ceased.

"You'd better show your front," said the Duke coldly, "or I shall kill you."

There was a sudden thrashing of the underbrush, and a small figure staggered out into the clearing beside the stream. Big brown eyes glared out of a face crowned with a tangle of golden hair which had been pulled about by the owner's passage through the brush. The Duke was pleased to observe the little maiden who had perched on the wall yesterday. Her gray gown was the worse for wear, but her hair, even though adorned with twigs and leaves, made a charming frame for the exquisite face.

"Well met, Queen Titania," offered the Duke with his most coaxing smile.

This flattering reference was not well received. Instead of blushing and stammering, the girl said sharply, "If we are to match names from Shakespeare, sir, allow me to tell you that you put me strongly in mind of Bottom the Weaver! Otherwise, after your aggressive behavior yesterday, I might have been tempted to call you Captain Hackum!"

The Duke took a more careful look at the furious girl in front of him. This time his expression was guarded.

"If I have offended you, little one, I am sorry for it," he said softly.

Belinda, her wrath checked as it were in mid-gallop, stared at him with suspicion. It was hard for her to read his handsome features; he stood very much at ease, watching her solemnly. The girl's slender brows drew together.

"You are very discreet today, sir! What has happened to the impudent bravo who charged the wall?"

A sparkle appeared in his eyes, although his countenance remained sober. "I thought, then, that I was responding gallantly to an invitation," he confessed.

Belinda gasped. "You presume, sir!" Then, finding it impossible to resist, she spoiled the effect of her haughty rebuke by asking, "What could have given you such an outrageous idea?"

The creature pretended an embarrassed reluctance to speak.

"I asked you a question, sir," the girl reminded him icily.

"Well," he began, his eyes bright with contained laughter, "perhaps it has slipped your mind that there was quite a—display of beautiful—uh—bare limbs—?"

"*Oh!*" Bright color rose in the girl's cheeks.

"Do you know how enchantingly pretty you look when you blush?" Now the audacious creature was openly laughing at her.

"No—that is—no one has told me—" began Belinda, even more adorably confused between pleasure and annoyance.

"The men of Sayre Village must be the greatest slow-tops in nature," suggested the man in commiserating tones.

"But I have not—that is—" the girl realized the folly of continuing such a conversation and drew a deep, steadying breath.

"I have come to visit the gypsy encampment," she said, primly.

"An excellent idea," the man approved. "So educational! May I have the honor of escorting you? But first—" he pursed his lips disparagingly.

"What is wrong?" the girl queried.

"You have twigs in your hair, and your gown is sadly untidy," the Duke informed her with a chuckle he could not suppress.

Belinda, shocked out of her bemused fascination by these rude comments, snapped, "And you, sir, have a damned dirty shirt!" in a tone which evoked for the Duke memories of dress parades and displeased senior officers. He took a closer look at the angry little figure before him, the tousled golden hair, the wide lovely brown eyes, the arrogant tilt of the chin. There had been the quick riposte to his Shakespearean gambit—surely a maid-servant wouldn't have known...? The small hands now clenched into fists were white and well cared for.... A staggering suspicion entered the Duke's mind. In spite of the outgrown gray dress and the sturdy shoes, this vision of beauty was neither the hoyden nor the servant she appeared. Frantically he tried to recall what Freya had said about the Earl's granddaughter. Blond, beautiful, with a startling openness of speech resulting from her grandfather's upbringing.

"Belinda's not mealymouthed," Freya had informed him, chuckling. "Some of our high sticklers censure her, but the young men adore it."

At the time, the Duke had frowned fastidiously and added it to his list of grievances against the girl. But now—could this rather grubby-looking little beauty be the Honorable Belinda Sayre, granddaughter of an Earl, and the woman he was expected to marry?

"If not Titania, by what name may I address you, nymph?" he asked, the smile which had won favor with some of the best-guarded hearts in Europe on his lips.

"I am—uh—Prudence Oliphant," replied the girl, presenting such a self-conscious mien that the Duke's suspicions were in a fair way of being confirmed. "A distant connection of the Sayre family," she added hastily.

The merest hint of a smile teased at the Duke's lips as he considered the disheveled little figure confronting him. "The family is not in residence, I take it?" he queried mildly.

A wild-rose blush suffused the girl's cheeks. "Oh!—You mean the—the informality of my costume?"

"That, too." The big man spared her nothing. "Unless, of course, they use you as an—ah—unpaid drudge? And you are forced to wear Miss Belinda Sayre's outgrown clothing?"

"Miss Belinda would not be caught dead in a dress like this," gritted Belinda.

"Ah! A haughty piece, is she?" commiserated the exasperating creature. "Niffy-naffy?"

"On the contrary," snapped the girl, "she is all affability! A most obliging and amiable disposition!"

"Indeed?" commented the man, viewing this information with a maddeningly incredulous air.

"And what the devil business is it of yours what Miss Belinda is like?" the girl bristled.

"No wonder the family rusticates you at Sayre Court," said the Duke, and now his smile became a mocking grin. "The style of your address is hardly suited to an elegant London drawing room."

Belinda's hand flashed up to slap the mocking face above her. With a rapidity which shocked her, her wrist was caught and held in a crushing grip.

"Oh, no, little spitfire! You must learn to

conduct yourself with more propriety! Shall I school you, I wonder!" and he looked down into her furious countenance with a kind of grim amusement.

Outraged, Belinda gasped. "What can a dirty gypsy tinker know of gentility?" She shrugged to free her wrist.

With embarrassing ease the man captured her other hand. "More than you are presently demonstrating, little termagant," he answered quietly. "Yes, I think it might amuse me to see if I can make a lady out of such a harum-scarum little maiden as Miss Prudence Oliphant."

Belinda glared up into the stern, handsome face. "I wish my—I wish there was a *man* here—!"

"There is," her tormentor said softly. "Oh, believe me, there is!"

For the first time in her pampered life, Belinda had an odd feeling which seemed to be compounded in equal measure of terror and delight. Unable to sustain the man's penetrating glance, she lowered her gaze to his broad chest and waited for his next move. After a moment he took both of her wrists in one large hand and with the other began to pluck the leaves and twigs from her hair.

Belinda found herself standing with unexpected docility under his ministrations. Even when he began to smooth and arrange her tumbled curls, she did not offer protest.

The man, releasing her wrists to give himself two hands for his work, shot her the occasional wary glance, suspecting a trick. At length his heartwarming smile appeared.

"Much better!" he said gently.

"My appearance?" challenged the girl, glancing up at him swiftly.

"Your behavior," he corrected her. "I am coming to believe that with some careful training, you might learn to go on quite acceptably in society," and he bent and placed his lips firmly upon her open mouth.

Belinda decided afterwards that it was shock which held her immobile beneath that attack, conveniently ignoring the fact that she had responded to the unexpected pressure by going up on tiptoe and leaning closer to the man's broad chest. With lightning speed she was clasped strongly in two powerful arms and fitted against a hard body. In order to facilitate this maneuver—and since she had really no place else to put them—Belinda placed her arms around the firm column of the man's neck and held on.

She had need to. The pressure of firm male lips against her own was creating some interesting new feelings inside her. One or two of the more dashing of the young officers who paid her court had attempted to steal a kiss under circumstances suitable for the performance of such tactics, but while Belinda, quite naturally curious, had permitted a chaste salute, she had held her defenses and remained in complete control of the exercise. This embrace was as different from those tentative maneuverings as brandy is from milk. Feeling a little dizzy, Belinda pulled back.

At once the grip on her loosened, and an unwelcome coolness struck that part of her chest which had been pressed to the man's.

"I just wanted to catch my breath," she found herself explaining, and moved back to him.

He threw his head up with an involuntary crow of laughter. "'Prudence'? Little one, you must not give yourself away so clearly! You should be all offended consequence, no matter how much you enjoyed my behavior!"

Belinda frowned. "Why?"

The man regarded her with such amused delight that she caught her breath. He kissed her once again, a soft touch quite unlike his earlier demanding pressure, and then said quietly, "To protect yourself, of course."

"You mean that men will regard me lightly if I make it too easy for them to kiss me?" she asked, belatedly recalling some of Lady Tulliver's endless homilies.

The man met her eyes, all traces of amusement gone.

"I think that some day soon one man is going to value that eager response above all else in the world. It will be all the more precious to him if it is for him alone."

Belinda pondered this dictum. "I believe you may be right," she admitted finally. "For I know *I* should feel most annoyed to discover that—that he was going around kissing dozens of other girls."

The golden eyebrows cocked wryly. "Surely not dozens," he objected. "Let us grant the fellow some discretion."

"Why should he be permitted to make love to even one girl besides me, if I am not to love anyone but him? It is not at all fair play!" protested Belinda with some heat.

"Before he has met you," offered the man more slowly, "perhaps he will not have realized what a—a delightful gift Fate has in store for him."

"But after he has met me," concluded Belinda happily, "of course he will never be tempted to kiss any other girl at all!"

"He would be a fool if he wished to," agreed the man.

A very satisfactory response! Belinda beamed up at the strong, handsome, faintly smiling countenance. The Duke caught his breath at the sheer enticing loveliness of the girl's face. "I think," he said hastily, "we should go to the camp, for that is where you were headed when we met, was it not?" Then, observing the look of disappointment which crossed the lovely little face, he added, "For Miss Prudence Oliphant, being a poor relation, must be particularly careful she is not discovered alone in the woods with a—'dirty gypsy tinker.'"

Belinda met his gaze with honesty. "I should not have said that to you. I was angry, but that is no excuse. I ask your forgiveness, sir."

"Bravely spoken," the man told her. "I accept your apology." He offered his arm. "May I have the honor of escorting you, Miss Prudence?"

As she placed her fingers correctly on his forearm, Belinda wished that she could hear this man say her own name in that deep, caressing voice.

# Chapter 11

The first gypsy they encountered as they entered the clearing was the girl Lara. She flashed a hostile glance toward the Duke, and then subjected Belinda to a contemptuous scrutiny. Before she could address them, however, the two Gorgios were surrounded by a ring of teasing young children and younger women, eager to welcome the pretty stranger. The Duke was surprised to notice that all the men save The Whip and Quebracho had disappeared, but concluded that the missing men were poaching or off collecting kegs of run brandy from wherever they were hidden. No doubt the residents of Sayre Court and the guests at The Climbing Man would soon be enjoying a very special tipple.

Dane introduced Belinda to the inquisitive group with a casual "This is Miss Prudence Oliphant."

The Whip advanced, Quebracho smiling at his shoulder, toward the newcomers, but before Anton had a chance to speak, Lara said with an abrupt laugh, *"Elephant?* What kind of name is that?"

Belinda, who had been hoping that none of the older women would recognize her as the Earl's granddaughter, drew herself up at this piece of gratuitous insolence. Quebracho offered a placating remark, his eyes on Belinda's face, but Lara continued scornfully, "Is *this* your mort, Gorgio? Now I see why her father had to arrange a match for her!"

*Oh, no,* groaned the Duke, *not that again!* Cursing himself for having used the truth as an excuse to get out of a tight place, he turned swiftly to his companion, noting her shocked surprise. Quickly he seized her hand in an ardent clasp.

"Although I had not had the pleasure of meeting her until today, I can only give thanks for my good fortune in being pledged to Miss Oliphant." Bending his bright gold head, he raised the small hand to his lips. At the same time, he pressed the girl's fingers in urgent warning.

Belinda, who had no notion why this attractive stranger should be telling such a monstrous whopper to his gypsy friends, was quick to realize that the encounter had developed a threatening aspect. The girl's suspicious glance, the old man's anxious friendliness, and the guarded look her companion was giving her suggested danger as much as the gypsy girl's attack had done. She looked at the giant gypsy who was approaching them. Was it not—? Yes, it was the same big fellow who had been so obsequious at the wall. His flat black gaze now held a darkly menacing challenge to the man beside her.

Belinda was not the Earl's granddaughter for nothing.

"My guardian wishes us to sign the marriage contracts today," she supported the golden-haired man's lie, "but I wanted to meet the friends with whom my promised husband had traveled into Devonshire." She smiled enchantingly at the leader of the gypsies. "I did not know, when I saw you all arrive in the village, that my intended was with you. I suppose he had come that way to get a glimpse of what the Fates had in store for him," she grinned saucily at the Duke. "I suppose I must thank God fasting that he did not turn tail and flee when he saw me!"

The gypsies chuckled, relishing the joke. The suspicion began to fade from the giant's face. Then Lara put in, waspishly, "But he didn't know you were the elephant when he saw you perching on your wall, did he?"

Ignoring this completely, Belinda smiled around the watching circle of gypsies. "You must introduce me, *darling*." The man did so, and Belinda said what was proper and gracious to each one, accepting their congratulations, and unconsciously enacting the role of great lady so well that Bracho was not the only one of the older gypsies who began to look at her consideringly. The Duke suppressed a grin. Finally Belinda turned to him.

"Now I think it is time we returned to— uh—to the house, do not you—*darling?*" and she pulled her fingers from the crushing grasp he had not relaxed.

"Indeed, sweetheart, you are right," he said, and flashed a lightning glance at her in which she read unholy amusement. The next instant he had taken advantage of her request by placing his arm around her waist and guiding her out of the group. "Yes, sweetheart! I wish above all things to have our affairs quickly settled." This was uttered with such prim complacence that the girl longed to deliver him a blistering setdown. Her eyes flashed him a promise of the reckoning to come, but she held the smile on her face as she accepted his guidance.

"I'll just pick up Ben from the line as I leave," he called softly to the now-grinning

Bracho. "My thanks for good company on the road!" His wave embraced them all. "Kushti bok!"

Belinda waited until the three—man, horse, and girl—were well out of sight and hearing of the camp before turning a wrathful face upon the culprit. The Duke forestalled her attack.

"Thank God you were so quick off the mark in apprehending a dangerous situation—and so cool in handling it!"

The warmth of his commendation momentarily checked her anger. "Dangerous?"

"Very. The chief was just looking for an excuse. He's never forgiven me for beating him at his own game when first we met upon the highroad. I believe he had decided not to let me leave without a mill."

"You must tell me the story some day," Belinda said coldly. "But surely there was the little matter of the girl, also?"

The Duke nodded. "He is beyond reason jealous of Lara. She is his chosen bride, but she is a minx and has been doing her possible to rouse his jealousy."

"Of you?" challenged Belinda.

"I was a honey-fall for her," the Duke admitted with a grin. "A stranger to the tribe— a Gorgio—my credentials and business unknown to them—above all, no one to report my loss if The Whip decided I was a serious rival for the girl's affections."

"Which, of course, you had made not the slightest push to win," added Belinda, a shade waspishly. She had been very well aware of the vicious look Lara had given the fair-haired man as they entered the camp. It had been neither provocative nor languishing— surely not anything to rouse anger or jealousy in even the most possessive of husbands-to-be! Had there been some other cause for the obvious animosity exhibited by the gypsy chieftain? Could the attempt at seduction have come from this man rather than from Lara? That would explain her angry revulsion. Belinda felt she must have time to evaluate the story her companion was telling her. Time, and more information.

"Is there in truth a girl living hereabouts to whom you are pledged—or was that a Banbury tale to discourage Lara?" she asked.

To her surprise, the man said, "Yes, there is," and then fell into a maddening silence as they wended their way along the shady path through the Home Woods.

"Well?" persisted Belinda. "Does she live in Sayre Village?" Rapidly she catalogued the unmarried girls of suitable age in the neighborhood: the Vicar's three daughters (well, four, if you counted Miss Amelia, but she surely was a little too long in the tooth to suit so handsome a man); the Doctor's lovely Cleo, perhaps a shade too young; Lawyer Morris's only child, Mary-Joan, but she was plump and carrot-thatched as well—oh! she was forgetting Squire Highcastle's daughter Helen, a beautiful dark-haired girl of sixteen. Would the Squire have countenanced so gothic an arrangement for his daughter with this gypsy rogue? But he wasn't a gypsy, whatever else he was!

"What is your name?" she snapped regarding the creature's innocent expression with a frown. "I cannot be forever calling you *'You'!*"

"Peregrine—er—Random," offered the Duke hopefully.

"Ridiculous," said the Earl's granddaughter shortly.

"Would you say 'ridiculous'?" protested the creature.

"It means wandering haphazardly," said the well-educated Belinda, "and is obviously an assumed name. *No* person is named Wandering Haphazardly."

"I recently heard of a man whose father called him Waiting-for-the-Light," argued the Duke, "and another named Parsifal Galahad. Of course *he* joined the army as Peter George. One cannot quite blame him."

"That," remarked Belinda austerely, "is quite another matter. Peregrine Random has a distinctly theatrical flavor."

The Duke was tempted for a moment to pursue this fascinating alternative, but decided the role of a traveling actor might be too fatiguing to sustain. Instead he offered, "My mother was a romantic?" with the air of one defending *à outrance* an untenable position.

"You are a Banbury man," accused the girl, "and you are enjoying all this too much for it to be a serious problem to you!"

The Duke's lazily provocative smile was wiped suddenly from his lips, and he stared soberly at the delightful little face under the tumbled golden curls. "On the contrary, Miss Oliphant, the problem is a most serious one, and my peace of mind—to say nothing of my future happiness—may well depend upon the events of the next few days."

The impact of this sudden gravity, combined with the Duke's undeniable virility and masculine beauty, struck Belinda with the force of a thunderbolt. She had had nothing in her life to prepare her for this man. Her grandfather had been middle-aged when she first became aware of his part in her life. She had never really known her father. The young sprigs of fashion she had met in London were either titled youths or dashing junior officers, not mature and sophisticated men of the world like the Duke. The Honorable Belinda Sayre had been carefully protected from such as these—partly by her youth, and partly by the efficient system of chaperonage perfected unobtrusively by her grandfather and Lady Tulliver. Now, her velvet brown eyes wide with concern, her cheeks pink with unaccustomed emotion, she scanned the handsome face above her.

"Are you in trouble?" she faltered. He could have lost his fortune at the gaming tables— she had heard of such things happening. Or he could be in one of those mysterious scrapes the young officers were frequently alluding to and always refusing to discuss with her. That would explain his traveling with a band of gypsies rather than by more conventional means. She scrutinized his rather grubby clothing. It seemed to her untrained eye to have been at one time of good quality, if a shade exotic. The short green velvet jacket and the silk shirt were really not the usual wear for Englishmen, but the riding boots— and Belinda did know about well-made boots— were of excellent style, although dreadfully in need of polish. And the stained buckskins fitted the man's strong, well-muscled thighs as though they had been made for him.

Belinda's cheeks grew even rosier as she raised her eyes to encounter his knowing gaze. It was essential to remove that warm, intent look from his face. The general's granddaughter attacked.

"I think you are cutting a wheedle, sirrah! You do not appear to me to be concerned about anything more serious than another man's girl!"

The Duke at once favored her with a delightful smile. "That, my child, can mean more trouble than you could dream of! But you must allow me to keep my guilty secret, Miss Oliphant. It would not be to my advantage to disclose it at the moment."

Belinda could think of no way to pursue this engrossing subject. They continued to walk along the path. After a few minutes the man said, "I shall be putting up for a few days at The Climbing Man, Miss Oliphant. When I have—uh—brought my costume into conformity with the polite mode, may I have the honor of calling upon you at Sayre Court?"

Belinda's gaze flashed up to the smiling countenance of the *soi-disant* Peregrine Random. "Why, *yes!* That is—no! I am not sure..." she hesitated, estimating the amount of conniving and explaining she would have to do to bring Dittisham and especially Mrs. Mayo to accept the grimy, enigmatic character beside her with any degree of equanimity.

The Duke, fully aware of Belinda's dilemma, took an unholy delight in the situation she had landed herself in. "I see what it is," he said, in tones of chagrin. "You are not allowed, in your position as distant connection of the family, to invite a guest. Are the Sayres so high-in-the-instep?"

"Of course they are not!" cried the Honorable Belinda.

"Then it must be myself who is an unworthy guest?" prodded the Duke, trying to look wistful and put-upon. He must have succeeded, for Miss Sayre was understood to say that, for her part, she would be very pleased to welcome Mr. Random to Sayre Court whenever he chose to present himself.

The Duke hastened to secure the territory he had won. "Then I may do myself the honor of waiting upon you as soon as I can correct the deficiencies of my wardrobe?"

"Yes, of course!" said the beleaguered Belinda, with the feeling she had been outmaneuvered.

Once again the irritating creature grinned at her. "Thank you! At that time I shall endeavor to explain to you the rather odd circumstances in which you found me—"

"That will be quite unnecessary," interrupted Belinda. She was already fabricating plans for explaining his presence to Dittisham, but took time to raise her brown eyes to his face with a smile that would have done credit to a dowager hostess of the *ton*. "Why do you not bring your fiancée with you, sir?" she asked graciously. "She resides, I collect, in the district?"

The Duke, becoming momentarily more enchanted with his future wife, was at pains to admit that, yes, his fiancée resided in the district, and that he hoped indeed that sh'

133

would be with him when he called at Sayre Court.

These civilities concluded, the couple found strangely little to say to one another as they approached the boundary of the Home Woods. Belinda was hoping that no employee of the Earl would see her with her raffish companion, for they had all known her from a child, and felt privileged to make impudent inquiries into her actions. The Duke, for his part, had begun to wonder just how long it would take to get his portmanteaux and his valet down from London. What with one thing and another, the abstracted pair walked so slowly that Ben, a most sagacious and long-suffering beast, was finally constrained to nudge his master quite sharply. Since he nudged him toward Belinda, the gentleman blundered against the lady and was compelled to throw his arms around her to prevent her from falling. This position was found to be unexpectedly comfortable by both parties, and after a long moment of staring rather foolishly into one another's eyes at close range, it seemed the most natural thing in the world that they should place their lips together.

A satisfying interval later, the Duke lifted his head. He was feeling dazed. He had kissed some of the most beautiful women in Europe, and been kissed by them in return, but not one of those admittedly pleasurable embraces had had the effect upon him of this simple pressure of lips. He had never experienced this tingling of every nerve in his body, this swelling sense of joy, this really remarkable hunger for more of the same pleasure. *By God!* thought the Duke joyfully, *I had no idea how soft and sweet a woman's lips could be!* And he looked at the soft red mouth, lost in wonder.

Under that bemused stare Belinda felt color rising in her face. For a timeless moment she had felt quite dizzy and wondered if she were going to swoon and miss the rest of this enchanting procedure. Her eyelids closed over the brown eyes. Unlike the Duke, she was not dazed. When they had kissed before, it had been a discovery, but this second kiss was much more. It came with such a sense of *rightness* that the shock of it sharpened Belinda's whole life into focus. That the man was promised to another, that she herself faced an arranged marriage, became at that moment irrelevant to the feeling of wholeness, of fated completion, which the touch of mouths had announced. She opened her eyes and looked, as if for the first time, at the man's face. Golden locks fell casually across a tanned forehead; clear gray eyes looked out at her from beneath sun-bleached eyebrows. A haze of dark golden beard glistened on his unshaven cheeks, but that did not in the least put her off. An arrogant straight nose, firm, well-cut lips, and a strong jaw completed an attractive male countenance, one schooled to self-discipline, the girl realized, and accustomed to keeping its own counsel. Belinda's gaze returned to the gray eyes, trying to read the man's nature and character. It seemed to her that although he was a stranger she had known him forever.

She thought, with a new wisdom she did not question, that the sense of recognition she felt must be love. She was, however, enough her grandfather's pupil to understand the nature of an obligation. The man had confessed to a contract with a local girl. In her own case, there was still the agreement between the Duke's father and her own. Such commitments must be honored; she had grown enough in the past week to understand that. So this walk through the woods, with the sunlight slanting tenderly through the green leaves and all the delicate scents of summer in the air, could well be all she would ever have—an hour out of time. It did not occur to Belinda that the man might have experienced a blaze of enlightenment similar to hers. She said, very softly, "I would like to kiss you once more—for farewell, Peregrine Random," and put her two small hands gently on either side of his face and drew it down to her lips.

The Duke accepted the embrace as though it were an accolade, holding his leaping senses in iron control and keeping his arms at his sides.

Belinda drew away. "Please bring your fiancée when you come to Sayre Court," she said. "She will be welcome."

# Chapter 12

Belinda made no effort to get in touch with Peregrine Random in the following three days. She knew she must come to terms with the extraordinary feeling she had for the wayward gentleman before she met him again. In accepting the fact that no future was possible with him there was pain, but the sense of sweetness in knowing that he existed in the world, and was well and happy, seemed to balance the feeling of loss.

Perhaps, she thought hopefully, I am growing up?

The new feeling of maturity and calm renunciation was rudely challenged on the third day, however, when the hubbub which inevitably heralded the arrival of the Earl brought her posthaste from the dining room into the central hall. Her grandfather, looking dusty, haggard, and angry, was demanding of Dittisham if Miss Belinda was still in residence, and being quietly assured that she was, when his eye lighted upon her, and the fierce old countenance assumed a reddish hue.

"There you are, Miss! No apologies for the bother and embarrassment you've put me to? No compunction for Lady Freya's distress, or the Tulliver's consternation?" He flung his riding coat in the direction of one of the footmen, his hat toward another, and his gloves, with remarkable restraint, he handed to the waiting Dittisham. "Well, Miss? Cat got your tongue?"

The new Belinda went toward him in a little rush and clasped her arms around his lean, upright body in a tight hug. Under her hands, she felt him tremble, and her heart was pierced by love and remorse.

"Dearest Grandy, I am so very happy to see you again! Do come in, and let Dittisham bring you something to play off your dust! You look as though you had ridden hell-for-leather all the way from London!"

"Fine language for a well-brought-up young lady," blustered the Earl, but the sullen red was fading from his cheeks, and a tentative ghost of a smile tugged at his lips. He peered down into the lovely face raised to his, noticed

140

the absence of the signs of grief he had dreaded to see, and with a feigned reluctance put his own arms around the laughing girl and kissed her on the cheek. "Playing the old man up sweet?" he challenged. "Well, Puss, better open the budget at once, and confess what fresh mischief you've been up to!"

"I have been most circumspect," protested the girl. She led him by the arm into the library. Settling him in his favorite chair, she nodded to the relieved Dittisham. "I'll be bound His Lordship hasn't broken his fast today, rushing pell-mell from the City to rescue me from God knows what! Ask Mrs. Mayo to send in a cold collation—"

" 'Cold collation'!" uttered the Earl in scathing accents, then grinned reluctantly at the two beaming faces before him. "You are a minx, Puss!" he complained as Dittisham bustled away to carry out his duties. "Why did you leave me? And more important, have you come to your senses?"

"Oh, yes!" The new Belinda forced herself to hold her temper in check at this unflattering if accurate question. Then, to divert his attention, she informed him that the gypsies were back in the Home Woods. "You'll be enjoying some excellent brandy with your dinner tonight."

"Don't try to put me off with gypsies and run brandy," snapped the Earl, sniffing a diversion. "What new imbroglio have you gotten us into?" A horrid suspicion struck him. "You haven't been encouraging some local beau out of spite?"

Belinda decided that her grandfather's uncanny perceptivity would have gotten him hanged as a warlock a hundred years earlier; it was deuced uncomfortable now. Seeing the growing alarm on his face, she attempted to make a recover.

"Local beau, Grandfather? You know the roster: Squire Highcastle's oafish heir and Cleo Mannering's red-headed brother! Which of them would you choose as a husband for me?"

"Neither, Miss, since you are already promised—" began her irate grandparent with parade-ground volume. Then he seemed to shrink a little. His voice, when he continued, was lower and, to Belinda, pitifully milder. "No, child, I'll not force that issue upon you again. Romsdale's behavior has been such as to disgust any person of sensibility." Then, catching a certain well-known set to her lovely chin, his glance sharpened. "The Duke has not waited upon you here, has he?"

Belinda shook her head. "No, he has not. But *I* have been thinking that my behavior was equally reprehensible. I behaved like a hurly-burly miss, rather than a Sayre. Running under fire! A craven performance!" She drew a steadying breath. "Perhaps we might endeavor to patch up the business—?"

142

The Earl frowned portentously. "You are telling me that you would be willing to forgive and forget—to swallow that fellow's insults...? I had not thought it of you, Belinda."

"I have come to believe that I acted like a spoiled and wilful child," confessed Belinda.

"And Romsdale behaved like an insufferable popinjay!" shouted the Earl, his loud, clear tones augmented by his sense of outrage.

It was perhaps less than fortunate that Dittisham had just opened the door and now announced, "His Grace the Duke of Romsdale!"

Belinda, shocked at the shattering possibility that His Grace had heard the Earl's comment, was still entertained by the horrified expression on her grandfather's face. She so far forgot all sense of decorum as to succumb to a desire to giggle. But when a tall, elegantly groomed gentleman entered the room on the heels of Dittisham's announcement, all impulse to laugh suddenly evaporated. For the visitor, point-device in the latest fashion, his blond hair attractively arranged, his handsome bronzed face imperturbable, was none other than Mr. Peregrine Random of the Open Road!

The Earl, having no knowledge of the meeting in the Home Woods, recovered his aplomb sooner than did Belinda. His advance upon his guest was more belligerent than courteous. "Well, sirrah, what do you want?" he snapped.

My Lord Duke, recognizing the authentic Sayre tone and idiom, hid a smile and said suavely, "I have come, sir, to pay my regrettably tardy respects to my future wife. Also to apologize for behavior which was insufferable, rag-mannered, arrogant, and considering the charm and beauty of my fiancée—damned stupid. Is it too much to hope that you might forgive such a cloth-headed simpleton as myself, sir? And ma'am?"

This last was said with such a beguiling air that Belinda felt her heart thump in her breast. Her mind was reeling with surprise and conjecture. The man before her, however elegantly turned out, was far from the pompous popinjay she had supposed the Duke to be. Somehow the image of a fascinating haphazardly wandering Gorgio had to be united with the persona of a noble diplomat—and at the moment, Belinda was not sure she was capable of making the meld.

Her grandfather seemed better able to accept the metamorphosis. But then he had probably not seen Peregrine Random, and had only the Duke's change of attitude to adjust to. The old man was walking toward the visitor with hand extended in welcome, his gust of rage as quickly burnt out as it had

flamed up. He said, with a wry smile, "Bid ye
welcome, Romsdale. It seems we may all have
been hasty!"

To which the Duke, clasping his hand
warmly, replied with obvious relief, "Or, in
my case, delinquent, sir! May I venture to
hope that Miss Belinda will view my suit with
similar lenience?"

Belinda suppressed a gasp. This was carrying the attack into enemy territory with
the same daring and dash he had exhibited
at the wall several days earlier. Her thoughts
awhirl, she yet realized that when she had
time to catch her breath, she might find her
affianced husband a very attractive man—or
pair of men! Had he been aware of her identity when he saw her on the wall? Perhaps
the disguise of poor relation had not for a
moment deceived him? If so, his announcement to the gypsies of an arranged marriage...his talk of the girl to whom he was
pledged...referred to her! He had known all
the time. He had been entertaining himself
at her expense! Belatedly she recalled the
amusement in his face, the teasing note in
his voice. He had been laughing at her for a
gauche child from the start! Raising eyes in
which a small flare of anger was beginning
to sparkle, Belinda observed that even now
a barely disguised amusement lit his eyes and
tugged at the well-shaped mouth.

It was a challenge she was unable to resist

"Grandfather, you are, I am afraid, the victim of a bare-faced deception. This—*gentleman* is running a rig on you. He is one Peregrine Random, late traveler with the gypsy band at present in Home Woods. You will remember I told you they have been here for several days? I have met Mr. Random twice. He thought me to be a poor relation of the Sayres. He made—advances."

Frowning thunderously, the Earl stared from one face to the other. "Indeed? Is this so, sirrah?"

The Duke said formally, not smiling now, "Sir, may I urgently request the favor of five minutes private conversation with you?"

Giving him a long, cold look, the Earl said harshly, "It might be advisable. Follow me, Romsdale."

Watching with a naughty grin as the two tall men stalked out of the room, Belinda hoped that the Earl would not be too hard upon the Duke and wondered just what the latter would find to say to excuse his masquerade. The thought of His Grace being compelled to explain and apologize so tickled her curiosity that she went out into the great hall and listened shamelessly at the closed library door, to Dittisham's disapproval and the footmen's secret amusement.

Unfortunately she was unable to hear anything except the Earl's voice raised in what she took to be anger. She eased the door open a crack. The Earl was in parade-ground form.

"—yourself 'Peregrine Random'! If you had to travel incognito, Romsdale, that was a damned sickly *nom-de-guerre!* What kind of ramshackle game have you been playing with my granddaughter?"

The Duke, who had promised himself not to let the old tyrant ruffle his temper, was endeavoring to cling to this sensible resolve. "First I must admit that I behaved badly—"

"Correct!" agreed the Earl, too heartily.

Dane sighed. It was clear that the old stickler was going to exact his pound of flesh. The Duke spared an unkind thought for his difficult little love, who had deliberately pitchforked him into this mess. "I came down to Sayre Court to mend my fences, sir. I hoped I might persuade your granddaughter to accept me—"

"Under an assumed name?" snapped the Earl, who, as many a cursed-out subaltern had discovered, was awake upon every suit, and no man with whom to enter lightly into an argument.

Holding his temper with both hands, the Duke continued grimly, "I was convinced that I had behaved so offensively that Belinda would refuse me under my own name, so I—"

"Took the coward's way out?" jibed the old autocrat, unforgivably.

The Duke received this low blow with a stiffening of his back. "I had hoped that I might, upon closer acquaintance, persuade Miss Belinda to consider my suit more kindly," he replied in a voice even colder than the Earl's had been. "If, however, I have offended you and your granddaughter beyond forgiveness, there is nothing left but to rid you of my presence with all dispatch. You have my word I shall not intrude upon you again!"

Belinda, following the conversation with increasing anxiety—for it had not gone at all as she had expected—now experienced panic. Bitterly she condemned herself for her folly in bringing up the question of Peregrine Random. Had not the Duke come in his proper person, offering apologies, making overtures toward better understanding, even toward the marriage she now ardently desired? Whatever had possessed her to act with such petty malice? Would she *never* put aside childish ways? Well, now she saw what had come of it. He was going, coldly, in anger— the man she knew she loved. Impulsively she pushed open the door, almost hitting the white-faced Duke who was making his exit at that moment.

"No! You must not go!" Belinda cried, coming into the room in a rush.

"Miss Belinda," the Duke acknowledged her between set teeth. "My apologies for any offense I may have given you, and for this intrusion." He bowed formally.

"But it was not an intrusion, My Lord Duke," Belinda pleaded, "since I had invited you several days ago!"

"Under an assumed name," interpolated the Earl, unwilling to drop that bone of contention.

"Grandfather!" Belinda protested. *Now of all times, must he be so knaggy?* "I forbid you to insult my guest—"

*"You* forbid *me!"* gasped the Earl, outraged by what he saw as a betrayal from within his own camp.

They glared at one another, the girl's delicate jaw set as firmly as her grandfather's, brown eyes flashing anger into icy blue ones.

The Duke had witnessed this confrontation with strong disapproval. From the old martinet he had expected nothing less, but from Belinda—? What had happened to the charming, soft-voiced, pretty-mannered girl who had enchanted him in the wood, he asked himself, conveniently forgetting the rather acerb comments she had made upon occasion. He tried to break into the argument, but both the Sayres were in full flight of rhetoric and appeared to have forgotten his existence. Rousing to a fine fury himself, the Duke crossed the room and broke up the quarrel by the simple expedient of shouting, *"Be quiet!"* in a voice as loud as the Earl's.

149

Into the shocked silence which followed this command, the Duke continued more quietly, but even more bitterly than the contestants.

"When I tried to discuss the matter of the arranged marriage with you in London, sir, my domineering sister took over the conversation. This time it is your belligerent granddaughter who has interrupted our argument. What has become of gentle, conformable womanhood? Can we men *never* be permitted to conduct a quarrel in peace?"

The old soldier was much struck by this point of view, and after a stunned moment, was understood to agree that a debate between gentlemen should not be interrupted by even well-meaning females. This remark was naturally highly resented by the one female present, who took instant exception to such a fanatical, rude, overbearing, and unfair decision.

The Duke's patience, which had been sorely tried, snapped. Turning his shoulder to Belinda, he faced her grandfather with icy courtesy. "It may be possible to continue our conversation at a later date," he said repressively. "In the meantime, sir, I have the honor to bid you good-day—and my compliments to Miss Belinda."

Without a single glance at the girl, the Duke turned and strode to the door. This was swung open for his exit, Dittisham having been on the listen to the exciting goings-on within the bookroom.

A small silence followed the Duke's departure. Then the Earl, pale and frowning, turned upon his granddaughter.

*"Belinda!"* he began in a voice of doom.

But the girl was not listening to him. Whirling, she ran into the hall and up the great staircase to her room, the door of which she slammed with extreme violence.

The footmen exchanged worried looks. Dittisham could not find it in his heart to rebuke them.

# Chapter 13

Belinda stood just inside the door of her room, fighting back the tears that burned in her eyes. How dared he stride from the library, deny her the opportunity to share in the discussion? Did it not concern her own future? She was at once angry, remorseful, and miserably unhappy—such a woeful mixture of emotions as she had never experienced before. Overriding all else was the fear that she had lost her chance of happiness with the Duke by her intransigent behavior. What had he said? That first his sister and then Belinda herself had interrupted him when he was trying to resolve the problem of the arranged marriage. Could she ever forget the look on his face when he protested, "—can we men

153

never be permitted to conduct a quarrel in peace?"

The sense of what he had said suddenly struck her, and she began to laugh hysterically. Then, wiping her eyes, she set herself to thinking rationally about the hornet's nest she had stirred up. Even if the Duke and her grandfather reached some sort of agreement over the proposed marriage, it seemed to the girl that she had tarnished the shining beauty of the occasion beyond repair. Could she ever restore the warmth and sweetness of his smile as he asked for her forgiveness and said she was charming and beautiful? With a bitter sob Belinda began to consider what she could do to reverse the situation.

Of course, after two such dismissals as she had given him, she might well have lost the Duke's affection forever. Still, he had said he might talk to her grandfather later, had he not? Surely that meant he was willing to give the Sayres, *grandpère et petite-fille,* another chance?

It is to be feared that her chagrin at the heavy-handed manner in which she had dealt with the Duke's peace overtures caused Belinda to lose some of her newly found maturity. It had been an object with her not to allow the Duke to see how powerfully he affected her, yet she knew now that she must at all costs avoid further wounds to his pride, however her own suffered. How could she give him a hint that she cared deeply, that she regretted her foolish comments about his *nom-de-chemin?* Hastily she tried to recall all she had been told about her prospective husband. He was intelligent, brave, a great negotiator, and very proud. Having already deeply insulted his pride, to which other facet of his nature could she best appeal?

Unbidden, the memory returned of the gentleness of his hands as they groomed her for the meeting with the gypsies. She had not chosen to think about that, for the close personal contact had been disturbing to her, suggesting as it did the actions of a lover or bridegroom. For a moment she allowed herself to consider how delightful it would be to receive and provide such intimate personal attention...on a regular basis.

She was forced to take herself firmly in hand. Stop daydreaming, Belinda! If you do not come up with a successful recover, you will have lost all chance of becoming the wife of His Grace the Duke of Romsdale. He is not the man to accept humiliating dismissals in stride. Not twice!

What then? Could she go to him at The Climbing Man and beg him to forgive her, to carry out the contract? She thought about that for a long time. The plan had a simplicity which appealed, and yet it was so *final!* For if he rejected her appeal, it was the end of the negotiations. It would be mortifying, also, even if he did not refuse her. Was her pride to weigh heavier in the scales than her life's happiness? Getting up, Belinda paced nervously around her room. There was the matter of the attitude her action would create between them, the tone of their future relationship which would be set by her humble confession and appeal. Would the Duke value her less or more because of it? Belinda clasped her hands together in fierce anxiety. The most important thing in her life, and she had foolishly marred it! Could she set all to rights?

She sat down before her mirror and stared at the girl's face within it. How could she seek to know so complex and sophisticated a man as Osric Dane when she did not even know her own heart and nature after eighteen years? She only understood, in this dark moment, that she could never outthink or outmaneuver this brilliant, worldy-wise man. Her appeal, if she dared to make one, must be on a level far more primitive than argument, pleading, or negotiation.

What then was left? Emotion. The heart's true speech. Emotions changed, perhaps, but they were powerful if honestly acknowledged. Yet how could she go to this twice-rejected man and tell him she loved him? Would he not consider her a "schoolroom chit" who did not know her own heart from one day to the next. Worse, might he be correct in that evaluation?

Belinda squared her shoulders. An announcement of *her* feelings could be misunderstood or disregarded. What else had she to fight with?

The answer came to her as clearly as though someone had spoken to her. *She had the Duke's emotions.* If in very truth what he felt for her was love, then it was to that emotion she must appeal. If love was there, it must be made to declare itself. But how? Surely she couldn't just ask him if he loved her? Not after what had already happened; and not, surely, to a man of the Duke's worldly experience. He could easily lie, to save her face or to salve his own pride. Either way would be so much less than the shining truth she sought. What then?

The Duke was a brave man, a man of action and daring. She must appeal to his chivalry, allow him to act as his character dictated. So: in what way could she arouse his protective feeling for her—if he had any? Hastily she ran over the precarious situations in which she might be able to embroil herself with some way of informing His Grace of her plight. A runaway horse would not only be out of character (she was an excellent rider), but difficult to warn him of in advance. Images of fire, flood, and earthquake appeared, only to be rejected. It was too much to hope that man or Nature would cooperate in such ways—and again the chief objection—how to inform the Duke that Miss Sayre was in danger of being burnt, drowned, or swallowed up in time for him to recruit his forces, find, and rescue her? It would be in keeping with the image he undoubtedly held of her if she were to run away again, yet how could she do so in a way which would ensure the Duke following her? At this point he would be more likely to consider it a good riddance!

And then the perfect scheme presented itself. A wide smile broke across the girl's face. *Of course!* She got up, washed her face in cold water to remove the signs of tears, changed hastily into Prudence Oliphant's cleaned and mended gray gown, and prepared to leave her room. At the door she paused, considered, and returned to pick up her reticule. She stuffed it with a bundle of notes from her drawer and at the last moment snatched up a crayon and a piece of paper. Then she slipped out of the house and headed for the Home Woods, praying that the gypsies had not yet left.

# Chapter 14

The Duke had returned to The Climbing Man in no pleasant frame of mind. Pliss, his valet, was surprised, though of course he did not show it, to see his master returning so early from the visit to Sayre Court. Excellent servant that he was, he knew what his master had been about that morning and expected that the acknowledged suitor for Miss Belinda's hand would be invited to remain for a leisurely luncheon with his future wife's family.

The valet read the signs clearly as his grim-faced master stamped into the sitting room of the private suite. Pliss was prepared to receive a blistering order to pack for an immediate departure. To his surprise, no such order was given. His master threw himself down into a chair and stared grimly at nothing. Pliss tenderly rescued the elegant chapeau and gloves from the table on which the Duke had thrown them and retired quietly to order a glass of brandy for His Grace.

Dane found himself in a quandary. For the first time in a very successful career he felt at a complete standstill—*point-non-plus*. *Damn the girl!* Why did he have to fall in love, like any greensick youth, with a hoity-toity, hot-at-hand little beauty whose temper was as nasty as her grandfather's? *You will be properly under the cat's foot if you pursue this female,* he warned himself. *No need to rejoin the army! Your life will be a continual battle, day and night, with the warlike Belinda.*

She should have been named Boadicea, or Matilda, the mighty Battle-Maid, he thought sourly. He told himself he was ready to forget the chit, return to London, and put the matter in the hands of his solicitors. If the Sayres were so unwilling to ally themselves with his family, by God they could whistle for him!

Strangely enough, the Duke made no move to implement this most reasonable decision, but moodily accepted a glass of brandy the invaluable Pliss was silently proffering. After a few moments the warming comfort of the wine a little restored his temper, so that when he became aware of the bustle of a coach ar-

160

riving in front of The Climbing Man, and a
few minutes later heard a knock on his sit-
ting-room door, and the voice of one of the inn
servants informing Pliss that a lady had arrived below who wished to be brought up to
the gentleman's chambers, he even found
himself grinning a little. So she'd come after
him, had she? The Duke squared his shoulders and prepared to be magnanimous.

To the Duke's intense dissatisfaction, Pliss
opened the door a few moments later to Lady
Freya Goncourt. Dane rose to his feet, frowning. "Freya! What brings *you* here?"

"I am glad to see you, too, brother," chuckled Freya, permitting Pliss to take her cloak
and bonnet. "My luggage is being brought
up," she advised the valet. "Will you help my
maid to prepare a chamber for me?" Then she
turned to scan her brother's face. "Not successful, then? Too depressing for you, dear
Dane."

"Freya!" gritted her brother, then, meeting
her guileless smile, his clouded countenance
broke reluctantly into a smile. "I might have
known you couldn't keep your fingers out of
it! I suppose I dare not ask what shatter-
brained scheme you have in mind to set all
to rights!" Then, taking in her appearance,
he gave a smile of genuine pleasure. *"En
grande tenue!"* He made her a sweeping bow.
"You should teach other ladies how to travel
in a coach for days and arrive looking as

though they had just stepped from the hands of their dressers."

Freya smiled in response. "I thank you, brother-diplomat, but you shall not put me off with compliments, however delightful. I apprehend you have failed to persuade the little Sayre that you are the answer to her maidenly dreams?"

"How the devil did you know I had come here to do just that?" wondered her brother. "Say rather, however, that I've retreated temporarily from the battlefield to lick my wounds and count my losses."

"As bad as that?"

"She's a redoubtable little lass, the one our father chose for me," admitted Dane wryly. "I thought I had her secure, but her mischievous, ill-timed levity, her grandfather's vile temper—to say nothing of my own!—put us into a fresh brangle," the Duke confessed.

Freya's eyes were quick to read his expression. A sigh of satisfaction escaped her lips. "You are—reconciled, then, to the marriage?"

The Duke strode to the window and stood staring out into the street below. "Reconciled? I begin to believe I must put it a good deal higher than that. You see, I met the girl with both of us playing Incognito—" and he proceeded to tell his sister the story of his pilgrimage.

When he had finished, Freya nodded with deep satisfaction. "Well done, brother! You've won the child's heart as yourself rather than because of your title and wealth! 'Tis what I'd hoped for—"

"Do not crow too soon," the Duke advised her. "At the moment, the state of the battle may be considered a temporary cease-fire, nothing more! And I am not sure I wish to resume so onerous a contest!"

"But you think Belinda is pretty?" probed Freya, after the immemorial manner of sisters.

"She is beautiful," admitted Dane, in the time-hallowed manner of lovers.

Freya took a new tack. "I am inclined to agree with you, however, that she's too young, a little silly, a spoiled rustic miss who isn't suitable for a man of your age and experience. Not up to your weight—as Goncourt would have said," she ended hastily, blushing under his shocked glance.

"Goncourt would never in all his aristocratic life have given utterance to such a crudity," Dane advised her sternly. "I must caution you to mind your tongue, Freya, if that's any example of your usual style of discourse." Then he grinned. "You were trying to manipulate me again, madam! You'll catch cold at that. I beg you will permit me to know my own business and my own mind—"

"And heart?" the woman asked softly.

"And heart," agreed the Duke. "It's too early to say what will come of this, but I find that I have made up my mind—with your help, dear Freya!—to stay in the field for another few days to see what parley and negotiation can do."

"Spoken like a diplomat," applauded Freya, laughing. After a moment the Duke joined her, wryly.

At this same time, Belinda was approaching the gypsy encampment. To her dismay, there was not a single man visible, and most of the horses were gone. The women and children were busy about their affairs, aware of the girl hovering at the edge of the clearing, but taking no overt notice of her. At length Belinda walked toward the fire and greeted the older woman who was stirring something in a great iron kettle.

"I am Prudence Oliphant," she began with a pleasant smile.

A sharp voice spoke out behind her. "Oh, yes, the elephant," sneered Lara. Belinda turned to face her.

"I have come," she said, keeping her voice steady and calm with an effort, "to find out if any one of the young men would care to earn some money."

"Doing what?" asked Lara unpleasantly.

"I think I shall wait to ask them in person."

"You'll have a long wait," retorted the gypsy girl with satisfaction. "The men are all off running brandy."

There was a concerted gasp from the women. The oldest one came quickly over to Lara and caught her by the shoulder, muttering a command in the Romany *jib*. Lara shook the old woman away angrily.

"Don't tell me what to say!" she snapped. "I am The Whip's chosen wife, remember? I will speak to this Gorgio mort as I please. What can she do? Who would listen to such as her?"

There was a quiet-voiced interruption. "Can I do something to help you, Mistress Oliphant?" inquired Quebracho, stepping down from his caravan and walking toward her. His wrinkled face bore a smile of welcome.

Belinda turned to the old man with relief. "I have a very special task I should like one of your young men to do for me," she began. "If I might explain to you—?"

Courteously Quebracho led her to his van. All the women returned to their tasks except Lara, who flounced over toward the big, brightly painted wagon of the chief. Belinda accepted Quebracho's help in climbing into his home-on-wheels. The old man offered her a chair. Belinda looked around her. Everything was clean and neatly ordered. There was a faint, spicy odor in the air, and fairly good light from two windows and the open door. The girl sat down with a smile for her host.

"I must tell you that I wish two things, for

which I am willing to pay—this." She opened her reticule and held out the neat roll of bills.

Quebracho bowed slightly but made no move to take the money. "I think you want three things," he commented.

"Three?"

"Your two tasks—and silence."

Belinda nodded. "Yes, that is chiefly why I came to your people rather than trying to get a boy from the village. First, I need to have a letter delivered tomorrow afternoon to The Climbing Man. Second, I would like to have the help of one of your young men to lead me to the old fisherman's shanty at Spaniard's Cove tomorrow at dusk."

"I am afraid—" began Quebracho, frowning.

"Oh, I know it's used to store the run brandy and other things," she told him. "Everyone in the county knows that! You can tell your people that my plan has nothing to do with any of those—activities."

Quebracho was looking so worried that the girl hesitated. Then her face cleared. "Oh! I think I have it! Is the hut full of kegs at this time? Well, that is awkward!" She paused, trying to read the dark, wrinkled face. "I am expecting to meet someone, late in the evening, and I wished to appoint some place where we might be sure of privacy for a few minutes."

*By Dadrus and Dai,* thought Quebracho,

*what is the Earl's grandchild wanting with a secret place of assignation?* It seemed to him that he should not assist such a lunatic plan in any way, for the relationship between the irascible peer and the gypsies had been a long and for the most part amicable one, and he had no desire to betray such trust as the Earl had given the tribe. Taking a searching look at the lovely, determined face before him, the old man realized that there was little he could say to change the chavi's mind. She did not know him, but he had watched her grow from a laughing, spirited child to this beautiful, wilful young woman. He must try to protect her in whatever way he could. He stood a moment in anxious thought.

Belinda became conscious of his concern. The look he had on his face could have adorned her grandfather's countenance at a moment when he was viewing her conduct with disapprobation, preparatory to giving her a piteous appeal or a sharp setdown— whichever he thought would influence her most. She smiled at him.

"I'm really not going to do anything my grandfather would disapprove of," she said, hoping she was right.

His stern expression did not alter. "If you say so, Miss Belinda," he murmured, unconvinced.

Her brown eyes opened wide. "You *know*—?"

"Yes. And I am thinking what the Earl will say when he learns of this escapade."

"The person I am sending the note to is my affianced husband," the girl confessed. "He is very angry with me now. Oh, he has cause! I am just trying to—to..."

Quebracho's frown vanished. Even before he had discovered the real identity of Peregrine Random in the village last night, the gypsy had valued him as a true man and worthy companion of the road. From the style Romsdale had displayed, Quebracho knew he could handle himself well in a tight spot. Had he not dealt so smoothly with Lara as to prevent an open break with Anton?

"If it is the Duke you are to meet, I will help you," he said.

Belinda exhaled. Was there anything this gypsy did not know? Still, he was willing to help. "Thank you."

"Write the note you wish to have delivered. Then come here at dusk tomorrow evening. You will be riding?"

Rapidly the girl reviewed her plan. If there was far to go, it would be important to have her own mount. And the Duke was sure to ride to the appointment. "Yes."

"When you come, I shall have a boy to guide you," he told her.

"But where am I to go, if not to Spaniard's Cove?"

Quebracho grinned slyly. "In quite the

168

other direction, Mistress! You would not wish to be taken for a Preventive, I expect."

Belinda smiled back at the old rogue. "No more than you would, Old One," she said saucily.

Quebracho laughed.

"But I must know my destination, so I can name it in my letter," she persisted.

It was her intention to wait alone for the Duke at the rendezvous, some coils of rope artistically displayed, a single candle burning, and to inform him that her captors had just left on an unknown errand, that she had managed to untie herself, and that she was everlastingly grateful for his daring rescue of her person—after which she fully expected he would enfold her in his arms for another of those embraces she found so delightful. She sighed with pleasure at the thought.

"The place?" she repeated.

"There is an old farm a few miles west along the coast. At one time the Earl's bailiff used the barn as a storage for hay from the western fields. It has been abandoned for several years. I think no one would be likely to disturb you there." His expression became somber. "The boy will not wait with you, for I fear your man may come fighting, and I would not have anyone hurt. Are you sure you wish to wait alone in such a ramshackle old building? There may be rats!"

Belinda was uncertain whether or not he

was teasing her. She said with spirit, "Pooh! I am not afraid of rats—much! I shall light a candle."

"Be sure you don't burn down the barn," Bracho chuckled. He had decided to follow the girl at a distance, and wait until the Duke arrived to be sure she came to no harm.

Then Belinda was thanking him gravely. He helped her down from his caravan and escorted her back to the edge of the Home Woods.

Neither of them noticed Lara lurking at the rear of the old man's wagon.

# Chapter 15

The Random Gentleman and his sister spent
the next day resting and conversing, catching
up most agreeably on the great events and
petty happenings of the last few years. They
liked each other very well, for siblings, and
found much pleasure in each other's sharp
wits. To add to their comfort, the cuisine at
The Climbing Man was unexpectedly toothsome. It transpired, upon inquiry, that Mrs.
Appledore had a cousin staying with her, an
emigré, who was a truly remarkable chef, in
spite of a temperamental disposition to fly up
in the boughs at the slightest failure of his
assistants to anticipate his needs and inten-
tions. This evidence of foreign instability was
regarded with tolerance, since the training

he had had before his parents left France had made him something quite out of the ordinary for a small Cornish inn. Both Freya and Dane reveled in his skill, and he quite outdid himself with such knowledgeable and appreciative guests.

It was while reclining very much at their ease in the orchard behind the inn, blissfully dozing after a delicious luncheon, that a message arrived for his Grace the Duke of Romsdale. It was scrawled upon a scrap of rather grubby paper, and the hand was far from elegant. The spelling also left much to be desired. (Belinda had felt herself quite artistic at representing the style of the lower orders.) The note read:

> Milord duk—. We have Mis Olyfant. If you ar wisfull to see her agen, you mus cum to the hom wood tonyt at moonrise with a hunderd pounds for a ransum. Put it in the holo oke neer the old Farm wher you wil find a note tellin you wher Mis O is hid.

> A frend

Dane passed the note to his sister without comment. She read it and turned to him with an inquiring lift of one slender eyebrow.

"An obvious ploy of Belinda's," suggested the Duke. A small grin tugged at his lips. "Romantic little wretch!"

"Well, you must admit it is a romantic ploy," Freya said mischievously. "To bring you out in the moonlight, all aquake with fear for her safety, yet full of determination to rout her abductors!"

"Pure melodrama," agreed the Duke. "I'm far from sure I should indulge the little rogue. If her grandfather catches us at such a romp, he'll call me out on the spot. A very irascible old gent, the Earl!" He chuckled. "Still, it might be amusing... 'tonyt at moonrise'—" A look of such tenderness shaped his lips that his sister stared with pleased surprise.

"You do love the little minx, don't you, Osric? I had truly hoped that you might! She's a darling, divinely pretty, and full of sparkle! She'll never bore you, and with the proper guidance, which you can give her in the next few years, will make a most acceptable Duchess."

"In spite of her deplorable spelling?" teased the Duke. "How can you have the barefaced effrontery to make such a statement after scanning this wretched missive? She's more like to ruin my credit in every capital in Europe! Little hoyden!" But the expression in his eyes was more tender than Freya had ever seen there.

Being a wise woman, she made no further remark, not even to ask what he intended to do, although she was agog to know every detail. Instead she went to her room to let her maid prepare her for dinner.

The Duke repaired to his own bedroom. In spite of his initial amusement, he felt he should consider the proposed escapade carefully. He was less sanguine about the adventure than he had permitted Freya to assume. For one thing, there was no knowing how many, and what sort of persons his difficult little love had enlisted in her playacting. Also to be considered were the alarm and inevitable anger of the Earl when he learned of the charade. The Duke was not amused by *that* prospect.

"Little fool! She's bound and determined to bring me into a confrontation with the old tyrant! And there will be The Whip to contend with, if, as I suspect, she's recruited some of his people to aid her in this absurd game."

The gypsy chief could prove a more formidable opponent than the romantic little ninnyhammer could ever imagine. She did not know of the severe lack of accord which had created a tension between Peregrine Random and The Whip—a deep-seated, natural antipathy which could never be peaceably resolved.

"Oh, damn the little wretch!" muttered the Duke, changing, to Pliss's extreme displeasure, into the clothes he had worn while traveling with the gypsies. "If some of my friends in the embassies could see me now," he informed Pliss, "how amused they would be!"

"Incredulous, sir," amended the valet crisply.

The Duke shrugged, unable to defend his conduct in donning masquerade to please a wilful chit who had no idea of the risks she was causing them both to run.

He met Freya for dinner in the private sitting room of his suite. When he had listened for long enough to her admiring raillery at his costume, the Duke leaned forward purposefully. "I had better warn you, in case there is some hitch in this ridiculous charade, that the leader of the gypsy band, who bears the soubriquet The Whip, would as soon mill me down as look at me. His intended has been playing games to rouse his ardor, using me as the irritant. I will admit to you that I was happy to be able to walk out of the camp the other day without an open break."

Freya had stopped smiling. "Perhaps the gypsies are gone? Dane, you must not engage in fisticuffs with this man in a dark wood! After all, it is his native habitat, while you—"

"Of course I won't engage in fisticuffs—what a phrase!—if given any chance to avoid it! I don't really anticipate that Belinda has tried to enlist him in her scheme. Still, someone besides myself should know where I am going tonight, and be able to send out after me if I'm not back in good time—"

Freya had become pale and sober-faced. "I believe you had better tell me exactly what is going on," she said. "Under these circumstances, I am not all sure that you should indulge Belinda's playacting."

"I had the misfortune to best The Whip in a duel of wits when first we met—"

"Misfortune?" repeated Freya.

"As it now appears, yes. Had I permitted him to face me down, he would not have been left with this urgent need to prove himself superior in the eyes of his men. But *I* had to be the bravo-diplomat," the Duke said bitterly. "*I* had to live up to my inflated reputation and Conquer All. Perhaps this will teach me a lesson." He scowled. "The local Authority consists of one village constable whose most onerous duty is to keep an eye out for local poachers and strayed cattle. He is no match for even a gypsy brat, much less a determined and powerful adult."

"Should we inform the Earl?" suggested Freya. "It is still early evening, and Belinda will not yet have left the Court—" She regarded her normally self-confident brother with concealed dismay. The battle was not yet begun, and the Commander was in poor spirits!

"Would Belinda forgive me if I revealed her romantic game to her grandfather?" Dane asked ruefully. "She would think me a very poor imitation of a hero, in such a case."

Freya took a steadying breath. "You are underestimating yourself. The child has created an opportunity for you to rescue and claim her, thus putting an end to any further petty brangling about arranged marriages. In this way, all faces can be saved: the Earl's, yours, and her own, with universal acclaim to the hero of the piece. Do not tell me you cannot bring off a simple raid and rescue— you who received citations for courage and daring after Waterloo?"

The Duke put up one hand. "Spare me that," he requested, in so firm a voice that his sister held her tongue. After a moment's reflection, the Duke said slowly, "It may be that Belinda has not confided in any of the gypsies. Or if she has, it may be just one of the youths—or the girl Lara. I cannot count, however, upon any of them keeping this jest from the whole tribe. The People love an artfully contrived jape—some devious trick acted out for amusement or gain. I may find the whole tribe arrayed against me when I come— and for sure I will return with no money left on my person. But that would be acceptable to me. I might even enjoy it. What must not happen is a serious confrontation between the leader and myself. Pride would compel him to carry such a trial to...to a positive conclusion." He paused, already condemning himself for having been so open to his sister. Still, having gone so far, he must share the whole problem. "I should have to disable him, or permit him to disable me. An unpleasant choice."

"If I came with you," began Freya. "No, let me speak!" she insisted as the Duke tried to interrupt. "You could tell them that your sister had demanded to meet them all. It might become a social occasion? Perhaps if we brought wine, we might invite them to celebrate your engagement?"

While he completely refused to consider letting Freya accompany him to the Home Wood, the Duke liked her idea of making the occasion a celebration and had Pliss secure several bottles of the best French brandy host Appledore's cellars could produce. Then he had a dozen bottles of ale added to the collection and requested Appledore to secure the whole in Ben's saddlebags. For he had decided to ride to the rendezvous; Ben had saved his bacon more than once in the field and could be depended upon to help tonight if called upon.

So it was with lighter heart, and rather rueful amusement at his own behavior, that His Grace the Duke of Romsdale rode into the Home Wood well before moonrise that evening. It was the simplest of good tactics to pick a spot and settle in before the battle.

# Chapter 16

Belinda, escaping early after dinner by telling the Earl she had a headache, had dressed herself carefully in her best riding dress, a deep blue velvet which set off her lustrous hair. It was modishly tight at her slender waist, and modishly full in the skirt, and it was frogged à la Hussar. She rejected the plumed hat which was supposed to accompany it, but kept her whip and gloves. A purse? No, she'd already given Quebracho all she had left of this month's allowance. And well spent, she decided briskly as she prepared to slip out of the Court without attracting attention.

She was fortunate. The servants were at their own dinner, and the Earl would be drinking a glass or two of port in his library, a custom he had long enjoyed. Dull work sitting alone at table night after night when you withdraw, Puss, he had told her. In the event, Belinda did manage to escape to the stables without alarming any member of her too-devoted staff. Quickly she saddled her mare, Elba, and cantered off toward the Home Wood.

She had written the note telling the Duke that "Mis Olyfant" was tied up in the barn on the Old Farm near the highroad. This missive was to be left by Quebracho's agent in the hollow oak at the crossroads—a familiar local landmark. Now all that remained for her to do was to find her guide at the encampment and follow him to the dilapidated structure from which she was to be "rescued" by Osric Dane.

Belinda mused upon the name of her intended as she gave Elba her head to find a way through the woods in the dusk. The path was wide enough and well enough defined, even in the fading light, for the sagacious little mare to be able to make her way. Osric Dane. She was forced to admit that she could not care for the name Osric. Dane was better, and of course Romsdale carried its full measure of ancestral dignity. What should she be obliged to call him? Suppose, she thought with an urchin grin, she called him Perry, just to remind the arrogant nobleman of his ragtag masquerade? Would he be angry? She shivered deliciously. There was so much she had to learn of her future husband's moods, his preferences, his needs...With a sigh of satisfaction she contemplated the years ahead, so full of mystery and delight.

Just before she reached the encampment, she was accosted by a slight lad in dark leather clothes and the familiar broad-brimmed hat. The youth's face was darkened by charcoal. Belinda had heard from the servants at the Court that the smugglers often darkened their hands and faces at night so as to slip past the prowling Excise Riding officers.

"You have come to lead me to the old barn?" Belinda asked softly.

The lad nodded and, mounting a black mare, led the way stealthily through the forest. It was dark within the wood, and Belinda found herself completely disoriented. It seemed to her that they were proceeding south rather than west—still, she had not come this way before and had really no idea where the abandoned barn was located.

At length the horses moved out of the wood. When they had been walking across rough turf for several minutes, Belinda noted a lightening in the sky to the east.

"We are here," announced the gypsy youth, indicating a dilapidated-looking structure huddled among dark, looming rocks. Belinda hardly glanced at it. With a sense of surprise she found herself looking at a calm ocean gleaming faintly in moonglow.

"I thought we were to avoid the fisherman's hut? Quebracho said—"

"It is all changed," the youth said huskily. "Get inside quick, Miss. I am to tie you up."

The girl dismounted. "I do not wish to run afoul of the Free Traders," she began, dubiously.

The youth had already dismounted and was leading both horses around to the rear of the hut. In a moment he was back, working at the lock on the heavy plank door. The door swung inward silently, well oiled. Belinda followed the slim figure into the dark, redolent interior. She heard the scrape of flint. A dull, small flame of light grew in one corner of the shanty, revealing the fact that almost the entire space was piled with kegs.

"I am sure you have mistaken your instructions," Belinda began.

The youth, a dark silhouette between her and the soot-blackened lantern, was advancing toward her, a coil of rope in one hand. He dragged over a wooden stool. "Sit down, Miss. Don't be afraid. I will tie the ropes loosely." There was almost a sneer in the gruff little voice.

Head high, Belinda seated herself on the stool. "Get on with it," she said coolly, offering her wrists.

Instead of tying them, the gypsy looped the rope around her body, binding her arms to her sides. The rope was pulled so snugly that it cut into Belinda's flesh, but she scorned to voice an objection. When the knot was secure, the gypsy brought a long end up and tied it around Belinda's wrists in a complicated fastening.

"That is very uncomfortable," the Earl's granddaughter said quietly. "It need not be so tight, surely? 'Tis a trick we play, only."

Without replying, the gypsy knelt and bound her ankles. That knot was pulled painfully tight also. Belinda experienced a pang of alarm. The gypsy rose and stood, fists on hips, in front of the helpless girl.

"So, Miss Elephant, you are ready for your little performance. Scream, Miss! Bring your pretty man to your side! The Whip and nine of our best Roms are on the way here to move the brandy to a safer spot in the woods."

"But it's *moonlight!*" Stunned by the sudden hostility on the part of Quebracho's courier, Belinda could only grasp at the idea of how dangerous for the smugglers such a moonlit transit would be.

"Needs must when the devil drives," quoted the gypsy spitefully. "Not even a stupid exciseman would dream we'd try to move the casks tonight."

"But what has that to do with—with Mr. Random and myself?"

"We've had word your lover is a Preventive, on the prowl."

"That's absurd," snapped Belinda. "Mr. Random is no Preventive officer!"

"You'll swear his name *is* Random, then?" sneered the gypsy.

"He is—a duke," said Belinda fiercely. "You had better not try to harm him!"

"A duke!" There was a snort of mocking laughter as the gypsy turned away to check the smoking lantern. "He's a Customs Riding officer, trying to worm his way into the tribe!" But Belinda was not listening. Something about the bending, graceful figure had caught her attention.

"You—you're a girl!" she accused.

Lara came to stand in front of her prisoner.

"It took you long enough, Elephant!" Even under the film of charcoal, her features showed scorn. "We'll soon see what The Whip has to say to your lover's spying! He will catch you both here with the run cargo."

Belinda felt a tremendous sense of relief. "The Duke won't come here. He expects to rescue me from the Old Farm."

"And why should he expect that?" Lara's grin was a white slash in the darkened face.

"That's what my letter said—the one Quebracho left in the riven oak...."

Lara laughed. "But he can't find it if it isn't there, can he? A boy will tell him you are here, and lead him to you."

184

"I cannot believe Quebracho would—"

"Who said anything about Quebracho? I've diddled that old fool, too." Lara pulled a cloth from her pocket and whipped it around Belinda's face in a crude but quite effective gag.

"Just so you don't scream and warn your Gorgio lover away before The Whip finds him," she taunted. Then, extinguishing the lantern, she slipped out of the hut. Before she closed the door, Lara said, "Kushti bok, mort! That means good luck!" A key grated, there was the sound of hoofbeats...then silence.

# Chapter 17

Dressed in his new riding coat, one of Stultz's triumphs, and mounted on Ben, the Duke rode away from The Climbing Man in the dusk. His sister watched him from the window of her bedroom, smiling affectionately at the picture he presented. He had done the little Belinda proud, her gallant cavalier, and would surely satisfy her romantic young heart with his handsome face, fine carriage, and abundant charm.

The Duke, it must be admitted, was also convinced that he would impress his sentimental little love. He was resolved to be very gentle, very protective—and wondered with a rueful grin if she had also hired a bravo to let her hero demonstate his mettle.

Still smiling, he reached the barn at the Old Farm whose location he had had Dolby, his groom, discover from the inn ostler well before nightfall. In the dusk he made a careful reconnaissance of the building and terrain and found no evidence of any recent habitation or current preparations for a dramatic encounter. He brought Ben into the barn and put him well out of sight in the farthest stall. Then he essayed the rickety ladder leading up to the loft, found it barely climbable, and tested the flooring of the loft itself. It was in his mind that he might perch up there in a position to observe who entered without being noticed.

As the time passed, the Duke wished he had brought along the cigars he had at the last moment given Dolby to hold for him, thinking it would not do to warn the chit, or her supporting actors, if any, that he had already arrived by filling the air with the aroma of tobacco. He began to find the waiting a dead bore and was almost ready to climb down to investigate further, when one of the barn doors swung creakily open. At first the Duke could not make out who the newcomer could be. Then a lantern was lighted, revealing the figure of Bracho. The gypsy held the lantern above his head and called out quietly, "Miss Belinda? Are you here?"

A little qualm of unease stirred in Dane's mind. Rising, he leaned over the edge of the loft. "She is not here yet, Bracho. Are you her accomplice in this little scheme?"

Quebracho relaxed when he heard the note of amusement in the big man's voice. "Yes, sir, I am helping the little lady play her game. I might have known you would not be taken in."

"What is to happen now?" asked the Duke.

Quebracho stared up at him in the gloom. "She has not come to the camp. I was to lead her here, tie her up, and stay out of sight until you arrived, then slip quietly away. I thought perhaps she had ridden directly here."

Dane's feeling of alarm was stronger. "She did not come to the camp at the time arranged?"

The old man shook his head.

"Could you or she have mistaken the meeting place?"

"It is possible," admitted Bracho. "She had first intended to go to the fisherman's hut at Spaniard's Cove—but I thought I had persuaded her to change her mind. Still, she might have gone there by mistake."

"Will you tell me how to get there, and then wait here for her in case she has been delayed?"

The old man hesitated. "I would very much rather that it was I who went to the Cove, sir, and you who waited here."

"What is this 'sir'? Am I not your friend Peregrine?"

"I believe a *part* of that," smiled the old man. "But I repeat, friend, let me be the one to go to the Cove."

"What, and spoil the child's scheme?" protested the Duke. "What a dastard it would make me, to hang back while you effect her rescue! Why do you hesitate?"

"Because tonight Anton and some of our men are moving the brandy from the hut to a safer, less conspicuous place in the woods. I would not have them discover you while they are engaged in that activity."

"They might resent my presence," agreed the Duke lightly, but his feeling of alarm was stronger than ever. What would happen to the girl if she were discovered by a group of Free Traders, nervous at the work they were doing, and quite likely to strike before asking any questions of an intruder? And even if they realized the intruder was a girl, would they accept that she was the Earl's granddaughter and treat her gently? She had introduced herself to them as a poor relation of the Sayre family. Would that be enough to protect her?

The Duke made up his mind. Swinging down quickly from the loft, he walked over to where Ben was waiting. "Describe me this Spaniard's Cove, Bracho. Perhaps, if I hurry, I can reach it and make sure she is gone before your men arrive. Are you sure this is the night? I had not thought the Gentlemen went about their affairs in bright moonlight."

"It is because most people, including the Preventives, hold that very thought that The Whip has planned his move for tonight," grinned the old man. "It would be quicker if you took the highroad back to the camp. There, get one of the boys to lead you to the Cove. Tell him Bracho sent you to help. I'll wait here a little longer for Miss Belinda, then meet you at the Cove."

Quebracho congratulated himself on a clever solution. The boys in the camp would naturally offer all the delaying tactics possible, and Bracho would reach the Cove well before the Englishman.

They parted with mutual goodwill.

# Chapter 18

The Duke, very much on his guard, rode down
the track toward the ocean. He had not been
suspicious when, on arriving at the camp, he
had found a grinning gypsy boy waiting to
take him to the new rendezvous. The boy informed him that the lady had changed her
mind, and that he had been detailed to conduct his honor to the Cove. The Duke had
noticed, during the days that he had spent on
the road with the tribe, that this youngster,
a pert and cheerful rascal, had been frequently in mischief but never vicious or sullen. He was more than willing to accept the
lad as his guide. They had struck out at once,
the boy running ahead on foot, following a
path through the woods.

The Duke set Ben to a canter, reflecting with some amusement on the undeniable pleasure the whole race took in a trick. The more fantastic and absurd the prank, the better the gypsies liked it. Especially if there was money to be made! The Duke wondered how much his devious little love had given them to enlist their support in this ridiculous *espièglerie* of hers. It might be diverting to find out.

"How much did—er—Miss Oliphant pay you to lead me to her prison?" he asked, abruptly enough to disconcert a more seasoned campaigner than the boy.

The lad only chuckled as he ran tirelessly beside the Duke's horse. "Oh, nothing, your honor!" he retorted. "It is reward enough to serve so pretty a lady!"

"Sauce!" said the Duke. "I suppose I must ask one of your elders and betters, if I would get a sensible answer."

"Now that, your honor," panted the child, keeping up so gamely that Dane in very pity slowed Ben to a walk, "puts me in mind of one of our tribal stories. Would you like me to tell it to you?"

Grinning, the Duke took a coin from his pocket and tossed it to the boy, who caught it deftly.

"The story goes," the boy began gleefully, "that a fine gentleman—as it might be your

194

honor, sir!—asked twenty gypsies the same question, and got twenty different answers."

"That is a story?" mocked the Duke.

"Not all of it," chuckled the boy. "This noble Gorgio then asked *one* gypsy the same question twenty times—and still got twenty different answers!" He shouted with laughter.

"There is no doubt you were born to be hanged," said the Duke, also laughing, "and I should know better than to ask even one question of your supple-tongued race. I am surprised that Quebracho sent such a devious guide."

The small dark face turned quickly up to his. "Quebracho?" the boy repeated. After that he had nothing to say.

It was then that Dane became suspicious. It was a feeling he had learned to trust during the war, and later, in the course of negotiations with foreign agents. It was not always an infallible guide, but it had several times put him on guard in time to prevent a disaster or save a delicate situation. Yet when he tried to analyze it, he could discover no menace in the actions of the child. He was completely unable to accept that the gypsies had really kidnapped any member of the Earl's household, no matter how distantly related. The old general's writ ran strong in the county, as the gypsies knew, and in all England as well. Woe betide any man who harmed a member of that old fire-eater's family! Why, then, this warning sense of trouble ahead? The Duke began to ask himself if he had been a fool to come upon this romantic errand without even so much as a pistol for defense. Well, perhaps forewarned would be forearmed!

He frowned and reined Ben in when he came in sight of the hut among the rocks. The cove, so effectively sheltered between high cliffs, was a perfect spot for smugglers—or for an ambush. The sturdy little shed had all the marks of a depot, with its well-contrived air of disuse and dilapidation. And yet—the moon, now well above the eastern horizon, gave so much light to the scene that one could not imagine any clandestine activity succeeding. The Duke could have seen at a glance if ten men were milling around on the beach. There was no one in sight. The Duke shrugged and followed his guide toward the hut.

"I'll hold yer *groi*," offered the child, too eagerly.

"Ben doesn't take kindly to strange grooms," said Dane quietly. "He might savage you if he thought you were playing me false."

"I would just hold him ready for you while you unlocked the door."

The Duke rode right up to the heavy wooden door and bent to examine it. "There is a heavy padlock here. Do you not have the key?"

"No," the boy admitted. "Didn't she give you one?"

"She?"

"I mean—Quebracho."

Before the boy could move, Dane was out of the saddle and had him firmly by the shoulder. "I think we had better get this straightened out," he said softly. "And I am not asking you twenty questions! I am telling you to give me a few true answers to this wild-goose chase. Why is the hut locked? Is the Earl of Sayre's granddaughter inside? Have you Roms harmed her?"

After the last questions, the boy's face, which had been set in stubborn lines, suddenly appeared surprised.

"The old Tartar's grandchild? Oh, no, we'd none of us mess with her! There's only that silly mort who works in his kitchens, that came to see you one day at the camp—"

"That," said the Duke grimly, "was Miss Belinda Sayre, the Earl's granddaughter. I am asking you for the last time if she is locked in this hut, and if you have the key?"

Shock had driven all the mischief out of the boy's face. "No, sir, I haven't! Lara told me it was only—"

"Lara! Good God, what's she done to Belinda?" Loosing the boy, the Duke strode over to the door and wrenched at the lock. It was stout, and stoutly installed in solid oak. He looked around for a tool, a rock, anything to force it. The knowledge that the spiteful gypsy wench had maneuvered them all into this situation had shaken him. Congreve had said it: *nor Hell a fury like a woman scorned*—and Lara considered herself very much scorned. Not knowing the real identity of Miss Oliphant, the gypsy might have tried to do the other girl an injury. It must have seemed a perfect chance to get revenge upon a man who'd refused to play her little game—and in refusing, had left her open to humiliation in front of the whole tribe.

Frustrated, the Duke pounded on the heavy door. "Belinda! Are you in there?"

Man and boy waited, breath held, for an answer. For a long moment there was no audible sound, and then a pounding came dully through the wood.

"Hold on! We'll have you out in a minute!" The Duke ran over to Ben and led him right up to the door. Stripping off his own long, fashionable neckcloth, he threaded it through the hasp and tied it in a hard knot. He tied the other end to Ben's saddle. Mounting, Dane put the stallion into a slow pull. For an agonizing interval, nothing happened, and then the lock was wrenched out of the door. The gypsy boy cheered. Ignoring him, Dane dismounted, untied his neckcloth from the saddle and ran to push the heavy door open.

The inside of the hut was in total darkness. However, there was a muffled sound. The boy, hovering in the doorway, said quickly, "Bound to be a lantern here somewhere—smell it?"

"Get it," ordered the Duke, getting out flint and steel.

In a moment they had the lantern lit. "Still warm," the Duke said, and then he caught sight of the small bound figure of the Earl's granddaughter, and all else left his mind. Thrusting the lantern into the boy's hands, Dane reached the girl in two strides. He bent to undo the ropes which bound her, ordering the boy to bring the light closer. When nothing happened, he cast an irritated glance over his shoulder to discover the lantern reposing on the splintered wood floor and the empty doorway opening into the dark night. The boy was gone.

Smothering an oath, the Duke turned again to the business of freeing Belinda. First he removed the gag and was rewarded by a heartfelt rendition of his name. Both of them.

"Perry! Dane! I am so *thankful* to see you! You must leave me at once!"

Amusement warmed his eyes as he flashed her a glance before returning to the task of undoing the ropes. "If you are so glad to see me, in whichever role I am playing, why must I leave at once? Surely I may stay long enough to free you, little love, for I do not wish to insult Ben's rigid sense of propriety by carrying off a bound and captive maiden upon my saddle—or perhaps it would be more accurate to say, his saddle."

"Do not be a fool!" advised his little love severely. "I am trying to warn you that we shall be facing half the gypsy tribe within minutes—and they've been told you are a Preventive officer!"

The Duke's body tensed, but he continued to unwind the rope. "Is this so, indeed? Who can have given The Whip that particular piece of information?"

"Lara, herself, I should think—but where she got it, if not fabricated from sheer spite or an overactive imagination, I have no idea! You have been riding with them for days, have you not—masquerading, playing least-in-sight—I suppose a Customs Riding officer might have done something like that, to trap them at their smuggling. Why *did* you do it?"

"I enjoyed the freedom from responsibility," admitted the Duke. "Also I had to give myself some excuse for seeking out a maddening, autocratic, hot-tempered little wretch who has a habit of fleeing before a frontal approach—"

"You came down to Devon just to see me," breathed the girl.

By this time the Duke had freed her from the rope and was assisting her to her feet. From some cause, either that her muscles had cramped from the long confinement, or that she suffered a sudden weakness of the nerves,

Belinda found it expedient to lean against the broad firm chest of her rescuer. At once two big arms took her in a comforting grasp. This position suited Belinda more than she would have believed possible. She discovered a strong reluctance to detach herself from His Grace's firm grip. Fortunately, the Duke also displayed no eagerness to let go of his fragrant burden, and they stood closely clasped for some minutes. A belated sense of propriety moved the Duke to release Belinda and move a little away from her.

"Darling!" said the Duke, a trifle thickly.

"Darling!" answered Belinda, with a shocking lack of originality.

Where this pedestrian dialogue might have led can never be known, for at this moment there was a flurry of footsteps to the doorway and the voice of The Whip sounded in their ears.

"So we've caught you, have we? And with your doxy, by God!"

The Duke whirled, placing Belinda behind him, to find the doorway crowded with gypsies whose fiercely intent eyes held an utter absence of cordiality. "I am here with a member of the Earl's family—"

"Aye, we've heard that one," jeered The Whip crudely. "Now maybe you'll tell us what such a fine lady would be doing huddling with a bloody exciseman?"

Belinda chose this moment to come out

from behind the protection of the Duke's big body. There was a visible widening of dark eyes at the sight of her, even in the uncertain illumination of the lantern. Her hair glowed like guinea gold, but it was the expensive elegance of her velvet riding habit which opened the gypsies' eyes.

"I am the Earl's granddaughter," Belinda announced, for she had realized that her punctilious lover would never be willing to bandy her name and proper station about in a smugglers' den. The Whip gave a scornful laugh, but his men muttered and shuffled uneasily.

"You expect us to believe that?" jeered Anton, but there was doubt in his voice, and the beginnings of angry frustration. "Then my question stands, what is such a one as you claim to be doing *in secret* with a Preventive? Or shall I tell you?"

Dane growled deep in his throat, but the girl continued quietly, facing the silent gypsies rather than The Whip, "I assure you, men of Quebracho's tribe, that I am in truth Miss Belinda Sayre, granddaughter of the Right Honorable James Henry Darell ffoulkes Sayre, seventh Earl of Sayre and Wendover, your host in these woods for fifty years."

The Whip had hardly taken his eyes from the Duke, but he addressed Belinda with a sneer. "Do you tell me your noble grandfather condones your secret meetings with such raff

and scaff as this exciseman who is hiding behind your skirts?"

The Duke stretched out one long arm and
moved Belinda away from him. "Do not trouble to bandy words with this scum, Belinda.
Mount my horse and ride home at once."

The Whip's laugh grated loudly. "Are you
fool enough to think I'd let her run off and
bring you reinforcements?"

"Do you intend harm to Miss Sayre?"
snapped the Duke.

"No. When I've dealt with you, Preventive,
we'll escort the lady safely home to her grandfather."

"And how do you intend to secure my silence?" challenged the girl. "I'll see you all
in prison—"

"Belinda!" roared the Duke, giving her
such a glare as made her catch her breath.

Indeed, her threat had put a different kind
of tension into the group. The girl ignored it
as well as the Duke's warning. "Quebracho
knows I am here; Lara knows, for she led me
to this place and locked me in. My servants
know also—"

"Still," mocked The Whip, "I think few of
them would wish to spread the story of your
presence here with this exciseman. They will
wish to keep such a shameful escapade quiet,
will they not?"

"This gentleman is not a Custom's Riding
officer," the girl said quietly. "He is the Duke

of Romsdale, and my affianced husband—as we told you when we visited your camp."

Most of the gypsies had by now melted back from the doorway. They had not survived in foreign countries—and all countries were foreign to the Wandering People—by stirring up trouble with the ruling classes. Whatever the rights of this odd situation, it seemed to them that, first, this one man and girl, if released, were hardly likely to constitute an official threat to gypsy freedom or the run brandy, the couple's activities when first observed being of a totally different nature—and one they would be loath to flaunt. Second, they were both of that order which brooks no interference from less privileged persons. So with the wisdom of survival, they faded away from the danger and slipped through the woods to begin breaking camp. Anton would find a way to recoup their losses—it was the chief's duty.

The Whip was not willing to abandon either his brandy or his chance to punish the insolent Gorgio who had given him so much trouble. A duke? Even a babe at the breast would see the absurdity of such a claim! What would a nobleman be doing riding the roads with gypsies, or poking his nose into a smuggler's storehouse? He would choose a more comfortable place to bed his woman. The Whip, prey to strong and bitter emotions, was not in any case to think clearly. Lara had done her work too well. As had the Duke.

"There will be no crawling away this time for you, Gorgio. You will stay and take the punishment you've asked for. The woman may go or she may stay—to comfort the victor when I am finished with you—" he grinned the insult.

"She will leave at once. I shall see her mounted and safely on her way before I thrash you as you deserve," said the Duke, icily.

This moment of high drama was a little marred by a duet of voices as two bodies strove to enter the doorway at one time. The tangle resolved itself into the persons of Lara and Bracho. Both were shouting at once.

The old man got in first. "Anton, this is not Miss Oliphant—"

He was interrupted by Lara, shouting, "—this is a Preventive, Anton, don't let him trick you, he's—"

"—the Earl's grandchild. She plans to—"

"—arrest you for free trading—"

"—had a quarrel in London—"

"—that's why he came spying and joined the caravan—"

"—he intends to marry—"

"—me," finished Lara, having caught the gist of Bracho's last comment and using it deftly, "and be the new chieftain!"

"Shut up!" roared The Whip.

The Duke had not lost his poise, although rage glittered deep in the cold, gray eyes. "That was a little confusing," he agreed. "You should train your staff to make clearer reports. However, now that Quebracho is here, he can escort Miss Sayre back to the Court, while you and I finish our business."

This sensible suggestion found favor with no one but The Whip. He advanced further into the hut, his black eyes fixed on the Duke's face. Quebracho wore an expression of alarm, while Lara pouted with annoyance at the thought of being excluded from the scene of battle. Belinda, looking from The Whip's avid grin to the Duke's calm, unsmiling arrogance, tightened her lips. She was aware that the Duke was not best pleased with her interference thus far, and would probably have some pretty cutting things to say to her later, but surely it was too much to expect her to permit her newly acquired fiancé to be injured just to satisfy an incomprehensible and idiotic male ritual?

Quickly she glanced around the hut. There was no weapon at hand except the whip curled at the gypsy's belt. Silently she took two unobtrusive steps toward the keg upon which the Duke had placed the lantern. Then, noting carefully the position of The Whip, she stooped, picked up the lantern, and brought it down in a sweeping arc on The Whip's head.

Instantly the interior of the hut was plunged

into darkness. The Whip roared with pain and anger. The Duke called Belinda's name in a voice resounding with equal anger. Lara screamed. Belinda cried out because the handle of the lantern had been very hot indeed. Quebracho shouted to them to get out of the hut before it went up in flames.

This piece of advice was seen to be sound, since already there was an acrid, oily smell, and several tiny tongues of flame licked across the wooden floor.

"Get out before the brandy goes off!" yelled Quebracho. The Duke groped for and snatched up Belinda, hitting her head rather sharply with his own as he stooped to pick her up. Eyes watering, he made for the lighter rectangle of the open door with her. Lara had skipped out at the first hint of danger and was hovering several yards away from the now briskly burning hut, shrieking imprecations on everybody.

The Duke stumbled over the sand away from the hut, calling Ben to him. There was a neigh of alarm from the stallion at sight of the flames. Then hooves pounded in the Duke's direction. The Whip, staggering out of the shelter with a keg under each arm, tried to catch Ben's reins, dropped the brandy, and tripped over it. The great horse reared and trumpeted, striking out vicious forehooves. The Duke called him again, and Ben leaped toward his master. Tossing Belinda up over the saddle, the Duke threw himself up after her. He grasped the reins and, springing the horse away from the hut to be out of danger, wheeled to check that Quebracho and The Whip had been able to get away also. As he peered toward the flaming hut, the brandy kegs caught and exploded.

In the glare of light, the Duke was able to see that all the others were at least a distance from the flames, and running. Without another word, he wheeled the horse and put him to the path along which he had ridden earlier that night.

# Chapter 19

After several minutes of extreme discomfort, hanging with her head down on one side of Ben's back and her legs on the other, Belinda ventured a protest.

"This is very uncomfortable, Perry. Do you not think we might stop and—and—"

The Duke, still silent, halted and pulled her, rather roughly she thought, to a seated position before him.

"Thank you," offered Belinda meekly.

Still the Duke did not speak. Belinda began to have a fear that her champion might have resented her behavior in so summarily preventing the duel.

"He would not have fought fairly," she said,

low-voiced. "And he had a weapon, while you had none."

"I shall discuss this with you later, Belinda," said the Duke sternly. "Now be quiet till I get us out of the woods. I wish to be able to hear if we are being followed."

Feeling more miserable than she could ever remember, Belinda kept quiet for the next half hour. The bright moonlight was of some help to the Duke in finding his way, as it shone clearly through the trees and lighted the path except in the thickest groves. Finally Ben came out on the highroad. The Duke paused and stared around.

"We are within a mile of Sayre Village," Belinda said quietly. "To the right."

Still without speaking, the Duke turned Ben in the proper direction and put him to a canter.

Belinda began to feel very cross indeed. Well enough to enforce silence when they were vulnerable in the darkness of the woods, but here, on the road bright with moonlight, where any hostile approach would be clearly visible, surely the Duke should be willing to talk and to listen? Did the man not care how she herself had fared in the confusion of the escape from the hut? She might have been wounded! She *had* been, it came to her, feeling the pain of the burn she had received in lifting the handle of the lantern. Wounded in his service, and he not even concerned! She settled herself into her own resentful silence.

Within minutes they were riding past the inn. His Grace did not hesitate, but went on to the gates of Sayre Court. The gatehouse was quiet, and the man did not pause to alert the sleeping guardians. Instead he headed Ben directly toward the Court itself.

In silence the riders arrived at the great entrance. The Duke lifted Belinda down and steadied her.

"Can you get safely in without attracting too much notice?" he said coldly.

"I can," gritted Belinda.

"Good-night, then. I shall do myself the honor of waiting upon your grandfather tomorrow," said the Duke, and turning to Ben, rode quietly back toward the highroad.

Within five minutes Belinda was in her own room, having entered by a side door and crept up the servants' stairs. The bed, revealed in the light of a single candle, looked vastly enticing, but she had first to disrobe and tend to her burned hand. These tasks she accomplished quickly and at length crept into her bed with a sigh. After such a disastrous conclusion to her scheme for a romantic reconciliation, she had expected to lie awake—possibly weeping, for that was the present temper of her feelings—but within two minutes of touching her pillow, she was fast asleep.

The Duke was awaited at the inn. His groom lounged in the stable doorway, blowing a cloud from one of the Duke's cigars. When he heard Ben's hoofbeats on the highroad, Dolby hastily disposed of the butt and prepared to accept His Grace's horse. The Duke had nothing to say, and, sensing his mood, Dolby dared say nothing. When the Duke approached the inn itself, Pliss was there waiting to open the door and conduct him to his room, where a beaker of hot coffee sat upon the hob beside the fireplace, and his night robe and a pitcher of warm water were prepared for his comfort.

The Duke undressed in silence, sipped the coffee, and then commanded, "You will call me at eight o'clock in the morning."

Pliss nerved himself. "The Lady Freya is still awake, sir. She wished to be informed when you returned."

"Inform her."

"Will you speak to her tonight, sir?"

"No."

Pliss escaped the room thankfully.

# Chapter 20

The Duke's silence, so puzzling and deflating to Belinda, was at first mostly chagrin at the minor and unheroic role he had played in the evening's activities. Rather than rescuing a grateful and adoring girl, he had himself been rescued by her quick and reckless action in hitting The Whip with a lantern. This led to the realization that Belinda might have been injured or killed. The emotion he felt when he considered her rash behavior was not the complacent, slightly amused affection he had felt for a charming child-woman as he rode to the rendezvous. Instead he experienced a blazing anger at the impulsive, precipitate action which could so easily have resulted in serious injury for her, and this anger quite outweighed his resentment that she had usurped his role as the savior of the situation. The Duke struggled to keep his lips closed and his temper on rein during the long ride to Sayre Court, lest in his rage at her foolhardiness, he might do her an injury.

Even after his return to the inn, the chit safely delivered, his anger did not abate. When he thought of Belinda—and he found it impossible to think of anything else—he knew a strong impulse to turn her over his knee and give her a sound thrashing. How dared she risk her life in such a stupid, unnecessary imbroglio? Romantic rescue, forsooth! Involving a grown man in her silly fantasies! The Duke did not get to sleep until dawn was lightening the sky. And when he awoke, his rage, or whatever the uncomfortable emotion was, had not abated, but was, rather, exacerbated by his white night.

When Pliss ventured to wish him a good morning, he bit his valet's head off and was so uncivil to Freya that she gave him a thundering setdown. This did not serve to soothe his temper, and he departed for Sayre Court in a towering rage. Freya, watching him ride off this time, was gloomily convinced that something had gone very wrong with the romantic rendezvous, and that, in his present mood, he would assuredly ruin his chances for a reconciliation with the girl, to say nothing of her irascible progenitor.

The gatekeeper at Sayre Court did not challenge the Duke but bowed him through as though he had been expected. The approach to the great house was thought by connoisseurs to be particularly fine, but Dane had no eyes for sylvan glens, ornamental waters, or splendid plantings. Instead he stared ahead, absorbed in his own thoughts, allowing Ben to set his own pace through the golden morning.

Thus he was completely unprepared when a thin, vicious lash snaked out from the trees. It was aimed to circle his neck and pull him to the ground. Ben, however, not so bemused as his rider, sensed the attack from ambush, and leaped forward and to the side. The tip of the lash, instead of encircling the Duke's neck, cut deeply into his cheek.

Ben was already at full gallop, most properly removing his master from the site of ambush, but the pain of the cut, now bleeding profusely over the Duke's impeccable linen, released his demons. With a growl of fury, he pulled Ben about and charged the point of ambush.

Had Anton had two whips, the affair might have ended differently. While he was hastily recoiling his weapon, the maddening aristocrat was in front of him, bellowing insults.

"Come out, you sniveling coward! Show your front, you hedgehopping, back-stabbing craven, and I'll mill you to the ground!"

Such an invitation was not to be ignored. Snarling with rage, The Whip lunged into the road, all weapons forgotten save the primitive, original, most deeply satisfying ones.

It was a noble, an epic, encounter. Years later, recalling the fight with the wistful pride which comes with healed wounds and decreased ability, the Duke would wish that there had been a witness to the event, some knowledgeable bard who could have described the mighty blows given and received, the wily attacks and skillful counterattacks, the feints, the doublers, the trenchant hits and magnificent recovers. At the time, however, the Duke was too busy trying to kill his opponent before he himself was killed, to appreciate the science, skill, or pure savagery of the encounter.

Within a quarter of an hour the antagonists, bleeding, battered, and gasping for air, faced one another across two feet of open ground.

"Had 'nuff?" panted the Duke, wiping blood from his face for a clearer sight of his enemy.

"No," grunted The Whip through smashed lips.

"Good," gasped the Duke. How he was going to get his battered hands up and into action again, he had no idea. But the will was still there.

"—kill you—!" promised The Whip, glaring

through two blackened eyes. Then he collapsed very slowly, first to his knees, then prone upon the road.

"Well done," admitted the Duke, thickly, through numb lips, yet ever the sportsman. Then he called for Ben and leaned against the warm, steady flank until he could gather the strength to mount.

His arrival at the Court caused a considerable stir. The butler and all four footmen rushed out to aid the injured guest.

"My Lord Duke!" groaned Dittisham. "Who has done this to Your Grace?"

"Fellow's down in the road," Dane managed, through puffed lips. "—get him to gypsy camp—they'll take care of him."

Tenderly Dittisham helped the wounded man inside, got him seated, and, sending one footman for Doctor Mannering, dispatched another to fetch clean cloths and water and a third to inform the Earl his guest had arrived. "Though how we shall make you presentable, Your Grace, I have no idea."

The Duke indeed offered a shocking appearance. His shirt was soaked with gore; his coat, which in the heat of anger he had neglected to remove, was torn and split; his face and hands were rapidly swelling and darkening. Dittisham instructed a fourth footman to send a groom to The Climbing Man, there to request a complete change of clothing from

His Grace's valet, but the Duke counter-manded that order.

"Don't wish to disturb m' sister," he enun-ciated carefully. "Besides, m'business here will be brief."

These ominous words caused Dittisham, who, like all the servants, had a very accurate idea of what was going on between their mis-tress and this London swell, to experience a Sinking Feeling. Had the noble suitor lost his ardor? Dittisham was compelled to admit that his wooing had been, for the wooer at least, a stormy one, and that this latest setback would be enough to discourage all but the most lionhearted of swains.

While he was gently wiping the worst of the bloodstains from the ducal brow and cheeks, and tutting over the gash The Whip had cut in one cheek, Belinda and the Earl entered upon the scene, she from the stair-way, he from his bookroom.

Belinda was first to the Duke's side. Kneel-ing beside the chair in which Dittisham had placed him, she stared at his face with grief and pity.

"Oh, my dear heart, have I caused this to happen to you?" and bowing her head in re-morse, she clasped and held a corner of his coat, fearing to touch the injured hands.

The Earl, catching sight of the battered fea-tures, was not appalled. He had seen much worse damage in his time, and began by asking the Duke, on a regrettably jovial note, how his opponent had fared. The Duke rose to this, and was understood to say that he'd left him flat on his face in the road, from which place he had better be removed before someone drove over him.

Belinda, affronted by this levity in the face of the Duke's injuries, told her grandfather pretty sharply to bring Dane a glass of brandy. Dittisham had already seen to this essential restorative, and the girl was able to put the glass to Dane's lips most tenderly. He drained it and it seemed to put new heart into him, for he sat up and requested the Earl to grant him a few moments in private.

This did not suit the girl. She rose from her knees and followed the Earl and the Duke (supported by Dittisham and the strongest footman) into the bookroom.

"This is beyond anything foolish!" she began, shocked quite out of decorum by her fears for the Duke. "He should be lying upon his bed, attended by a physician! *Where is* Dr. Mannering? Has he not been sent for?"

"Quiet, Belinda," warned her grandfather. "Dittisham has sent round for him, I'll be bound. Now leave us, child, until he comes."

Belinda set her chin stubbornly, and got a firm grip on the Duke's sleeve. "No," she said firmly.

Dane, for his part, was feeling like a man who has just endured a brain-loosening, cheek-splitting, body-battering passage at arms with a more than worthy opponent—in other words, he was in no mood to observe the niceties of civil behavior. He was also deeply embarrassed at having to present himself to Belinda in his blood-spattered state—for not having seen The Whip, she might be supposed to think that the Duke had gotten the worst of the encounter. And after his airy assumption of the heroic role, it was deflating to be compelled to display himself in such a guise. For these and other reasons—his head was aching so badly his eyes felt as though they were crossed—the Duke's patience, never his strongest suit, and now, God knew, tried beyond endurance, snapped. Detaching his coat from Belinda's grasp, he rose unsteadily to his feet and faced the Earl with a military stance.

"*Sir!* Permission to speak!"

"Granted!" agreed the old General, recognizing the gambit.

"Request permission to deal with my future wife as I see fit. *Sir.*"

The fierce old eyes peered out from under the bushy brows, took the measure of the man, and replied crisply, "Granted."

The Duke turned, staggered, then seized Belinda firmly from behind by her arms and propelled her before him to the door. This was opened for him at the correct moment by Dittisham, who had been anxiously listening from the hall. The Duke and his unwilling companion passed through without pause, let, or hindrance. Under the fascinated eyes of the footmen, the Duke deposited the furious girl at the foot of the stairs.

"Go to your room, Belinda! I shall talk to you later," ordered her arrogant lover. Then he turned about and made his way back to the library, and if his step was not as steady as it might have been, at least his shoulders were held straight, and his head high. He closed the door after him with a firm snap.

It was a thrilling exit. The flame of outrage faded from the girl's cheek and a reluctant smile softened her lovely features.

"May I offer you my sincere congratulations, Miss Bel?" said Dittisham in a reverent voice. "If I may be permitted to say so, there goes a Nonpareil!"

Belinda chuckled. "I believe I shall find him adequate," she said softly. Dittisham and all the footmen joined in her laughter.

# Let COVENTRY Give You
## A Little Old-Fashioned Romance

# CLASSIC BESTSELLERS
# from FAWCETT BOOKS

☐ SELECTED SHORT STORIES OF
    NATHANIEL HAWTHORNE     30846   $2.25
  Edited by Alfred Kazin
☐ MAGGIE: A GIRL OF THE STREETS   30854   $2.25
  by Stephen Crane
☐ SATAN IN GORAY     24326   $2.50
  by Isaac Bashevis Singer
☐ THE RISE AND FALL OF THE
    THIRD REICH     23442   $3.95
  by William Shirer
☐ THE WIND     04579   $2.25
  by Dorothy Scarborough
☐ ALL QUIET ON THE WESTERN FRONT   23808   $2.50
  by Erich Maria Remarque
☐ TO KILL A MOCKINGBIRD     08376   $2.50
  by Harper Lee
☐ NORTHWEST PASSAGE     24095   $2.95
  by Kenneth Roberts
☐ THE FLOUNDER     24180   $2.95
  by Gunter Grass
☐ THE CHOSEN     24200   $2.95
  by Chaim Potok
☐ THE SOURCE     23859   $3.95
  by James A. Michener

Buy them at your local bookstore or use this handy coupon for ordering.

COLUMBIA BOOK SERVICE
32275 Mally Road, P.O. Box FB, Madison Heights, MI 48071

Please send me the books I have checked above. Orders for less than 5 books
must include 75¢ for the first book and 25¢ for each additional book to cover
postage and handling. Orders for 5 books or more postage is FREE. Send check
or money order only. Allow 3-4 weeks for delivery.

Cost $_____    Name_____

Sales tax*_____    Address_____

Postage _____    City_____

Total $_____    State_____ Zip_____

*The government requires us to collect sales tax in all states except AK, DE,
MT, NH and OR.

Prices and availability subject to change without notice.

**8195**

# CURRENT CREST BESTSELLERS

☐ THE NINJA            24367   $3.50
by Eric Van Lustbader
They were merciless assassins, skilled in the ways of love and the
deadliest of martial arts. An exotic thriller spanning postwar Japan
and present-day New York.

☐ SHOCKTRAUMA        24387   $3.75
by Jon Franklin & Alan Doelp
A factual account of the revolutionary life-saving techniques of Dr.
R Cowley. The authors investigate the methods, politics and profes-
sional ethics of Dr. Cowley's controversial medical center.

☐ KANE & ABEL          24376   $3.75
by Jeffrey Archer
A saga spanning 60 years, this is the story of two ruthless, powerful
businessmen whose ultimate confrontation rocks the financial com-
munity as well as their own lives.

☐ GREEN MONDAY       24400   $3.50
by Michael M. Thomas
An all-too-plausible thriller in which the clandestine manipulation
of world oil prices results in the most fantastic bull market the
world has ever known.

☐ PRIVATE SECTOR       24368   $2.95
by Jeff Millar
Two rival reporters (who happen to be lovers) are onto the same
story: a game plan of corporate terror and nuclear blackmail that
threatens the whole country.

Buy them at your local bookstore or use this handy coupon for ordering.

COLUMBIA BOOK SERVICE
32275 Mally Road, P.O. Box FB, Madison Heights, MI 48071

Please send me the books I have checked above. Orders for less than 5 books
must include 75¢ for the first book and 25¢ for each additional book to cover
postage and handling. Orders for 5 books or more postage is FREE. Send check
or money order only. Allow 3-4 weeks for delivery.

Cost $_____   Name_____

Sales tax*_____   Address_____

Postage _____   City_____

Total $_____   State_____ Zip_____

*The government requires us to collect sales tax in all states except AK, DE,
MT, NH and OR.

Prices and availability subject to change without notice.

8202